John Hodge is still [illegible] 's imagination has mov[illegible] first book published *The Fa*[illegible] new journey, in the form of his new b[illegible] *Gets Slimm*.

As always, this is for my wife, Yvette, she's been at my side throughout this book, my listening block. I've also had good support from John Stigwood, thank you John

John Hodge

The Fat Club Gets Slimm

They may have bitten off
more then they can chew

Austin Macauley Publishers™
London • Cambridge • New York • Sharjah

A CIP catalogue record for this title is available from the British Library.

ISBN 9781398424289 (Paperback)
ISBN 9781398424296 (ePub e-book)

www.austinmacauley.com

First Published 2023
Austin Macauley Publishers Ltd®
1 Canada Square
Canary Wharf
London
E14 5AA

Chapter 1

"We will be OK, won't we?" Summer said as she fastened her seatbelt. Even though she was excited by what had just happened, but nevertheless, her nerves were now beginning to show.

Simon took her hand and squeezed it to try and reassure her.

"We'll be OK. Don't worry about it. Teddy will look after us."

But the reality was, he didn't know either. Would the Fat Club look after them? Only time would tell.

Simon started the car and then thought to himself, The last time I was in this predicament was when they asked me to listen in on Mr Bay.

But now, it was him and his wife, Summer, and none of them knew what would be in store for them.

The drive back home was a long one, well, for Summer it was, on the other hand, Simon had done the journey so many times before it was now becoming quite tedious.

"So, what is Jessica like?"

This put Simon on the back foot. Where did that one come from. "Why do you ask?" he said as he turned the car music down.

"I just thought I would ask you because she's come up quite a few times in Teddy's conversations, and let's be honest, you've talked about her as well."

Simon could see where this was going and knocked it right on the head there and then, the last thing he wanted was Summer getting the wrong idea, he needed her by his side if they were going to get through this for the Fat Club, he told Summer what he thought of Jessica.

"At first, I thought she was quite a pleasant person, that was until I got to know her, but then when her smoke screen dropped I realised she was quite rude and condescending, and that was just the start of it, and then there's Rose." Summer said what Simon was thinking maybe it's a qualification you have to have for the Fat Club, they both nodded their heads at the same time. Hardly a word was said for the rest of their journey home. Simon tried to make light-hearted conversation, but it fell on deaf ears, although when he talked about the shopping spree, they were going to be going on Summer did cheer up a little.

They finally got home around tea time, Summer made her way up the stairs to the front door of the house whilst Simon put his car away. Once in his office, he noticed on his desk, the small, blue flashing light on his laptop indicating to him that he had mail, he knew straight away who it was from, and of course, he was right, the Fat Club don't hang around, they had sent him the dates with a full itinerary of what would be involved, plus a planned route and times of their journey to London. It was going to be by train with a car and driver ready and waiting at the other end to take them to their hotel. He printed the information off ready to go over it with Summer. Again, the evening was a warm one; there was a stickiness of humidity in the air that evening as they sat on their patio having olives and cheese and with wine, of course. Simon put the two pieces of paper on the table in front of Summer.

"This is our itinerary for the three days," he said as he gulped on his glass of wine as if it was water. Under the watchful eye of Summer who then gave him one of her disappointing looks. They were both going to be travelling down to London by train, on where a car and driver would be waiting to take them to the Goldson hotel where they both would be staying for two nights with three days shopping. They had separate timetables to keep too. Simon listened with his wine glass in his hand as Summer read them out loud.

"My personal shopper is a person called Miss Rebecca Parker, and yours is somebody called Mr Jonathan Dalton."

Simon gently teased the paper from Summer's fingers, sliding it into the centre of the table. "Let's not worry about this now."

Summer agreed with him. After all, the evening was theirs now, and as the wine flowed freely that evening and three bottles later, Summer became excited again, with the help from the wine, which rubbed off a little on Simon, however, Summer did go over the dates and times just one more time saying, "It gives us nine days to get ready for what is yet to come."

Little did they know, the shopping spree was just the start.

Nine days seemed such a long time away, but it was soon to be on them. Simon parked his car in the long stay car park at midland Central and boarded the train for London, but not before he checked over his car, taking pictures from every angle. Summer sat next to the window as Simon sat next to her opening his iPad, he was now in the stages with the leasing company. All his hard work had paid off and was just waiting for the delivery date. Summer gazed out from the window as the train pulled away slowly from the station and then passed through the busy industrial part of the city, it wasn't long before they were heading through the countryside destined for London, Simon had his eye on his watch, he had estimated the time travelling would be around two hours 20 minutes or there about. The rhythmic sounds of the wheels running along the tracks sent Summer to sleep, she could sleep anywhere, she always put this down to the long hours she worked. Time passed on as Simon finished his emails and was now waiting for the reply from the leasing company when he noticed the build-up of properties from the train window, as he looked down at his watch again, the train was running on time which made a pleasant change.

Just another 10 or so minutes to go before we come into the station. He gently tapped Summer on the shoulder. "We're here, we should be coming into the station in 10 minutes," he said as he stood up to get their luggage from the rack above them and then placing them on the floor in front of him, sitting back down. Simon waited as the other passengers got off the train first, rather than have the hustle and bustle of trying to get off they always thought staying in their seats and waiting was the better option. The different smells of perfumes and deodorants wafted across their nose, and every now and then somebody with a bad case of body odour would walk pass them catching them both out, it was now finally their turn to disembark from the train, the heat and the smell of the diesel engine was so overwhelming but then Simon said as he carried their bags to the exit. "The smell of the diesel engine is nothing compared to the body odour we had just experienced." They were both finally outside the train station where the driver of their car found them both.

"Your car, sir, madam."

Simon could only think that the Fat Club must have given the driver a description of them both.

"This way, sir and madam." He pressed his key fob and the boot opened as he put their cases into the car, he then opened the car door on the side of the curb so they could both get in, once they had settled down in the back the driver then introduced himself as Tony. "I will be your driver for the duration of your stay, but to which one of you, I'm not sure as there will be another car and driver at the hotel waiting for you, you will know more when we get there," he continued to say, "the hotel is less than five miles away, but because of the traffic it will take at least 30 minutes to get there, but I will endeavour to make your journey as comfortable as possible for you both."

The time passed as they sat there. To all, it was just another car on a busy road in the centre of London the dark tinted windows shield them both from onlookers as they both looked out, only Simon knew what was to come. They could see the Goldson hotel coming up in the distance, Tony looked back through his rear-view mirror. "This is your hotel. Please just make your way in and your bags will follow." As Tony closed the car door behind them, he touched a small microphone on his suit lapel. "They're on their way into you now."

As Simon and Summer walked into the hotel, they were greeted by a tall well-dressed man, who promptly took them to one side.

"Your room is ready for you. I have looked after your hotel reservation so please would you like to follow me." He walked them both to the lift, which was going to take them to the second floor, once in the lift, he never gave his name but did explain what was going to happen next. "Your room is ready for you both, however, there is a briefing you need to attend first, this will explain everything you need to know about your little trip you're both going to be going on, do you understand what I have just said to you?" They both nodded their heads.

"Good," he said as the lift door slowly opened. "This way then, please."

They followed him down the hall to the only door with a 'do not disturb' sign hanging on the door handle. A man standing at the far end of the hall nodded his head to him as he opened the door for Simon and Summer. Once they were both in the room, the door was closed behind them and then another door opened to reveal the person they were meeting.

"Good afternoon, Mr and Mrs Rodgers. I am your case officer. I will be in charge of this operation."

Simon put his forehead in to his hands and then looked up towards Summer. "This can't be happening."

Summer looked at him. "Why, what's wrong?"

Simon looked at Summer again, he hesitated and then said, "Summer, meet Jessica Green."

The hotel room they were in was full of splendour with expensive paintings hanging on the walls and high-class furniture filling the room, as you would expect from a five star plus hotel in the heart of London, but silence now filled the air now that everyone had been introduced to each other.

Simon and Summer sat together on one of the couches, a large Persian rug placed on the floor separated them from everybody, it felt like it was placed on no man's land, the second couch was precisely placed on the other side of the rug, and as Simon and Summer slowly sank down into it as they sat there waiting as Jessica Green walked around the room as if she owned the place.

"This is where we are," she said as she stopped to look out of the window. "As you know, and I know, Teddy has already put you partly in the picture about what's going to happen, well, now I'm going to tell you everything you need to know about the trip you're both going to be going on. Mr Slimm," Jessica Green then said it again, but this time slightly louder. "Mr Slimm is the head of the organisation, he has a group of people that run the business for him, we now know Mr Slimm has a set meeting every three months to go over particular topics, but more importantly, he shows up to show people he's still around and in control, this stops other cartels trying to muscle in on his business, as you know we now have new information as to where Mr Slimm will be having his next meeting from our agent who risked his life to get this information to us." Jessica Green then stopped walking around the room and sat down on one of the many chairs in the room still maintaining her distance from them. "I'll be honest with you both, I don't think you're up to this. I think it's too dangerous for you both."

Summer moved up to the edge of the couch, pushing and pulling herself on Simon to get there, and then in her strong and somewhat satisfying voice, knowing that finally this was her chance to tell her what she really thought of her.

"Who do you think you are? Why only recently you were a glorified tea lady, and from what my husband said, you weren't any good at that either."

Jessica Green shook her shoulders in disbelief as Simon once again put his head down in to his hands wishing the couch would swallow him whole. Summer had now got her point a cross; this was something she had always been good at, of course that was only if she felt somebody was being obnoxious towards her, tensions were now high between them, and there was definitely no love lost.

Simon put his hand up like a little schoolboy in the classroom to ask a question, the only reason he did this was to try and stop the bickering, but now all eyes were on him. Things were now beginning to calm down a little after their outburst Jessica started to talk about Mr Slimm and the key men in his ruthless organisation.

"Make no mistake. These are very dangerous people and the four that we know of, have killed a whole family because their son was on the take from another drug cartel, even one of his men shot his own brother dead to get to the top and show his loyalty towards Mr Slimm, so to say the organisation is run on fear is an understatement, now moving on to Mr Slimm, he sees himself as a bit of a catch, a bit of a lady's man, but in reality, the women live in fear of him because of the repercussions to themselves and their families." Jessica got up from her chair and started to walk around the room again.

Summer thought does this woman ever stay still.

Jessica continued to say, "The hotel where Mr Slimm will be staying is one of the finest on the island it is only for the very wealthy, he and his head men will be staying there for three days, yes just three days, although the villa he's staying at is heavily guarded and it's not that far from the hotel, he will be calling in at the hotel where he's holding meetings every day, we know that there's four meetings because of the information we received, but there could be more, that's all we know, so you see, this is why we are sending you both in two weeks before the meeting starts. That way, you will have enough time to get yourself noticed, you see we have to get you both noticed for this to work. As you now know you're both going in as Mr and Mrs Bay."

Simon and Summer nodded their heads, although Simon coughed nervously, showing his anxiety, remembering he's been here before.

"Your dossier will be in your room, both of you must read and mesmerise the information. It's important that you take on your characters for this to work. You're going to be staying for the three days in London and you'll be under the names of Mr and Mrs Hardmen. This is one of the many names that is under the cloak of the Fat Club, you'll be meeting your personal shoppers today and they will be advising you both, is that understood?"

Summer's ears picked up; this was more like it.

But she was soon to be knocked down again when Jessica said, "In the late afternoon, you will be going through more dossiers on the companies you own, this is what you both will be doing for the duration of your stay, any questions?" They both sat there, speechless.

"Good, you will now be shown to your room you have two hours before you meet your drivers. The agent outside will lead the way." Jessica then said not a single word she just turned and walked towards the door as from where she came from and then disappeared out of sight leaving Simon and Summer standing there.

The two agents in the room turned to them. "This way, sir and madam." Showing them the door, once out of the room they walked down the long hallway to the agent at the end who then escorted them to their room. If there was a smell of open space, then that's what Summer would have smelled as she opened the door to their room, it was huge it was that big it seemed as if there was a slight echo or was that in her mind but one thing she did know and that was it was unbelievable, and as the room before it was filled with virtually the same decor, it was to die for, for Summer this was what she had dreamed of everything was in its place champagne bottles filled the chilled cabinet and expensive bottles of liqueurs filled the cabinet on the other side of the room, every door Summer opened had a fantastic surprise behind it as they were all filled with expensive furniture and fittings, of course Simon ruined the moment by saying 'it must cost a fortune to stay here', Summer looked across at him, yet again he had put his almighty foot in it, spoiling the moment. The hotel phone rang, and Simon once again was saved by the bell. Of course, Summer answered it.

"Madam, your car is now waiting for you at reception."

Summer said, 'thank you' in her posh telephone voice and then turned to Simon.

"Car's at reception, let's get going and Simon, don't show me up."

They both made their way down to reception where the two drivers were waiting for them, of course, they knew the first driver as he was the one who picked them up from the station but the second driver, well they both knew him but couldn't put a name to the face but then it clicked, it was Charles the driver who took care of them at the Richmond in Highgate.

Summer walked straight over to him. "Hello, Charles. Are you going to be my driver?"

Charles felt a little uncomfortable his face bright red. "Well, madam, I don't really know."

"Well, I know," Summer said. "And I would like you to be my driver." She turned to Simon. "Are you OK with that?" she said, of course Simon was OK he wasn't going to say anything different was he, he just wanted an easy life, so that was that, Summer had got her own way again, they were now standing in the main lobby like a pair of holiday makers waiting to go out on a day trip but not knowing where it was going to take them. Summer stood next to the main desk waiting whilst Simon flick through the brochures for the hotel spa. Summer was the one who was eager to get going, eager to spend the Fat Club's money, whereas Simon was the one that didn't know what all the fuss was about. He looked around the main lobby and thought is this what money gets you. He looked at the different kinds of people that were walking in and out of the building not really appreciating anything it was normal to them nothing was any different to them, people were just stood around talking to each other. He stood there trying to put a value to the wealth when a man walked up to reception he didn't say not one word the person on reception answered him as 'my lord', she passed him the keys to the penthouse suite and asked if he had any luggage, he answered back abruptly, "They'll be with me shortly."

Simon looked at him, this was a lord but he had a check cheesecloth shirt and ripped jeans, and on his feet well, he had a pair of old trainers that should have been put in the dust bin months ago, and his is one of the wealthiest men in Britain, Simon looked over to where Summer was standing he could see she was in shellshock of this person, but before Simon could say anything Summer simply said, "Simon, not a word."

And with that thought in mind, he thought it best to carry on looking at spa brochure.

"Simon, Simon are you listening to me?" Summer said as she moved towards him. "Simon, like I said before don't show me up today don't be saying anything silly listen to what they have to say and please use your common sense."

They had been waiting in the main lobby for 20 minutes when Summer stood up from her seat.

"What is going on? Why are we waiting?"

The receptionist behind the desk explain to her that the traffic was bad at this time of day, just as she said it, the two personal shoppers walked into the lobby, they introduce themselves as Miss Rebecca Parker and Mr Jonathan Dalton, Charles took control and introduce Rebecca to Summer and Jonathan to Simon, hands were shaken as they were introduced to each other. Rebecca then said, "Let's start at the restaurant," to which Summer's eyes lit up once again. Charles and Tony then led them out on to the main street from the cool air conditioning hotel lobby and into the warm and humid air outside, Summer and Rebecca followed Charles and Simon and Jonathan followed Tony to their cars. Summer had asked why they were going to the same restaurant in two cars she couldn't get her head around it but the reason behind this would soon be apparent, unknown to Summer, Jonathan and Rebecca were going to be watching them both for their etiquette after all if they were going to pull this off then they had to start somewhere. Charles was leading the way to the Royal Chesterfield this was one of the best restaurants in that part of London. Tony following closely behind manoeuvring in and around the traffic they eventually arrived and pulled up outside the restaurant two perfectly small prune olive trees line the front door, gold leaf lettering shun off the front window which said the Royal Chesterfield. It looked expensive, and that's because it was.

Rebecca turned to Summer as Charles got out to open the door for them, she explained to Summer, "You will be taking Jonathan's arm for this meal. I think that's for the best as it would look awfully strange if you and I were to sit together and your husband and Jonathan were sitting at the next table, but again there was a reason for this." Simon met Summer at the front door.

"What's going on? Why are they splitting us up?"

Tony hadn't given him any reason he just said, "You're going to be eating with Rebecca." Again, he said, "What's going on did you know about this?"

Summer took his hand to calm him down. "Simon, don't worry, I'll be sat at the next table come on let's get in." The restaurant was and looked fantastic, to say it was white would be an understatement, there were white walls with gold coloured wall lights, the floor was white marble with a gold inlay, the tables and chairs were white with golden runners draped over the back of the chairs, the table service was gold plated everything down to the napkin holders, lilies were placed on the table in gold vase with their seeds cut out so nothing could drop on the table.

Jonathan and Rebecca led the way in and gave their names to the head waiter. Jonathan took hold of Summer's arm in a tender manner. Simon just looked at him, forgetting about Rebecca, he watched as Jonathan waited till the waiter pull back the chair for Summer and then only sat down after she was settled. As for Simon, he was already sat but then jumped back up when he had seen what was going on, but then it was too late Rebecca had already put her hand out in a refusal to accept his apology. Summer's evening was going like a dream, Jonathan was throwing compliments at her left right and centre, where as for Rebecca, on the other hand, was mortified, to her this was embarrassing, it was only when Simon explained by making it clear to her that this was not his world, he told her that he would normally be the one that would be driving these people to the restaurant, and then sitting outside waiting for hours on end, and then he told her, "I'm more embarrassed then you will ever be, but I'm willing to learn if you would show me the way forward." He carried on to say, "It's OK for Summer, she's more than happy in this world this is where she is most happy." Rebecca looked across to where Jonathan and Summer were sitting and yes, she could see she was comfortable with her surroundings.

She thought to herself, Jonathan had the easy option this time, but then Rebecca saw Simon as a bit of a challenge and, to be honest, she always seen herself as being more superior than Jonathan. "OK, Simon, I will show you the way as much as I can. That is if you're willing to learn in such a short time."

Simon rubbed his hands on his knees. "I do want to know how. I do," he said as he looked across at Summer.

"Then I will do my best with the time I have."

The meal finished on a high for Summer, Jonathan had enjoyed her company, there were only a couple of things he pulled her up on. All in all, it went quite well where as Rebecca, of course, did her best to pull Simon through it but gave him some pointers to get him on this way. As they walked outside, once again the warm air hit them, Charles and Tony stood at their cars with the door open and once everybody was in their place, they slowly but firmly closed them behind them.

Tony sat and waited for Charles to pull away. "Where to now, madam?" Charles said.

Rebecca answered him, "I think it would be nice if you were to take myself and Summer back to the hotel." She turned to Summer for a sign of approval.

Summer said, "Yes, please."

Chapter 2

"Oh no, my head," Simon said as he opened his eyes slowly, it was that sense of confusion, you know…when you don't know where you are the morning after. He turned his head to the side ever so gently only to see his darling wife Summer dribbling from her mouth, her makeup still on from the night before, he slowly turned back over to where his watch was placed on the bedside table, and with squinting eyes he checked the time, just gone six he really wanted to try and go back to sleep but knew they both had to be up and out in three and a half hours. He slowly moved his feet to the side of the bed and placed them on the floor as if he was stepping onto an alien planet for the first time. His head was throbbing a pulsating pain like he had never had before. What the hell have I been drinking, he said to himself as he manoeuvred his somewhat tired body to the bathroom. Opening three different doors along the way just to find it, and then finally looking in to the mirror sticking his tongue out and pulling down his eyelid to check the whites of his eyes, just the thought of putting toothpaste on his toothbrush made him gip but he knew it had to be done if he was going to get rid of the vile taste in his mouth, he could hear Summer in the bedroom moaning and groaning, he thought she must be feeling as bad as him, well he hoped she was, he turned the shower on and then placed his hand under it waiting for warm water to flow his stomach still rumbling with that empty feeling. He eventually put his aching weary body in to the shower and within 10 minutes he was out again, that's all he could stand, his head felt as if it was a tin roof in a thunderstorm.

Simon was now in his robe and sitting there on the toilet with the seat lid down his head in his hands when in walked Summer, looking like Dracula's bride he took one look at her and then started to laugh. Luckily for him, Summer found it amusing as well and started to laugh with him, turning to him and saying, "The Fat Club did say everything is on the house, didn't they? Only what we drank last night we could have bought a small car."

Simon looked at her in astonishment. "Please don't say that."

"Now, for some serious retail therapy," Summer said as they both arrived at the main desk in the lobby, and in good time but still feeling a little queasy with empty stomachs. All they had that morning was a cup of tea and a packet of bourbon biscuits from their room. They sat there together waiting for Jonathan and Rebecca to show their faces, they both walked in at 9:30 bang on time. As Simon would say, but truth be known, they were waiting outside for 10 minutes because punctuality was the name of the game, never be early never be late but always be on time, it was now Jonathan's turn to take the lead.

"Right, Simon, you're with me today and obviously Summer, you're with Rebecca. We will be visiting two designer shops and we will hopefully all be meeting up at the second one."

Their cars were outside waiting for them. Charles and Tony had their back doors open ready.

"OK," Rebecca said. "Shall we go?"

Simon and Summer got to their cars, still feeling lightheaded, Simon was off to Edwards, which was known for its stylishness menswear, which was frequently visited by the famous. Tony pulled to a slow stop outside and then quickly opened the car door for them, Jonathan then waited as Tony led the way walking in front of them both to open the tailor's front door.

Jonathan said in his bombastic way, "I will ring you when we are ready."

Simon didn't like this man's arrogance. He thought to himself, It doesn't take much to say thank you, and as Simon walked in to the shop he was moved to one side, again by Jonathan with his 'me first' attitude, Simon could feel his blood rising especially after yesterday when he was watching him chatting his wife up, what a pompous little ass he really is, all Simon could think about was what Summer said in the hotel, 'don't show me up', and 'behave yourself'. With that in mind, he took a deep breath and soldiered on, once inside, with the door now closed behind them, he looked around. He had never seen anything like this before this was all new to him. Any suit he owned were always off the peg and his shirts, well they were out of a packet, as he stood there a well dressed man appeared from behind the counter.

"Can I help you, sir?"

Jonathan once again introduced himself first and carried on saying, "My client is going away for 14 days and would like a complete wardrobe to accommodate him for that time." The tailor pulled on his tape measure that was hung around his neck, pulling it from left to right. "Right, sir, let's get down to business."

Jonathan explained what his client would like as Simon stood there gobsmacked as Jonathan began to say, "Five suits in a Dorchester weave with Haverstock lining for summer use, and all in pastel colours, two dinner suits." The tailor wrote this down in shorthand. "Seven evening shirts with five ties and two Dickie bows in black, plus ten short sleeve summer shirts, six pairs of summer shoes and three pairs for the evening." Nothing was left out, not even his underwear and swimwear this took most of the day.

Meanwhile, not so far away, Summer and Rebecca where just about to open the door to a very expensive and exclusive shop on Tavistock Road. In her head, Summer could smell the designer labels, she ran her hand along the top of the garments. As she walked to the lady assistant standing at the other end of the shop, Rebecca said exactly the same as Jonathan, "My client is going away for 14 days and would like a full wardrobe to accommodate her." The shop assistant bowed her head slightly and then looked Summer up and down, Rebecca assured Summer that everything was OK she was merely looking you up and down to get your dress size.

Jonathan now had Simon in a short sleeve shirt, just one that had been picked out for him to see how it looked on.

"Yes, we will go with that I think." Simon didn't get a say in the matter next was the dinner suits, Jonathan had the shop assistant bring five different suits out and placed them in front of the large mirror. "This is very important and it's crucial that we get this right. Jackets only, please," he said to the assistant.

Simon asked him why and wished he hadn't as Jonathan stepped back from the mirror undoing his jacket and then putting his hand on his hip telling him, "A man's appearance starts at the head and shoulders and then chest and body, is that not right?" He waited for Simon's reply as the shop assistant nodded his head in agreement Simon could only look on. After trying all five on, Jonathan decided to go for the second jacket. It was black and edged in black velvet. He also had one in royal navy. He then went back to the evening shirts. Summer was now in what she would call her candy shop, designer upon designer clothes filled the rails, Rebecca explain to Summer that she didn't have to go for a well-known designer. It's the designers that don't have to promote their label that's what you need to be looking for she explained.

"Remember you will be socialising with a higher class of people and trust me you will be noticed." Nevertheless, Summer found it hard to let go of this particular brand, to her it was like saying goodbye to a close loved one, Rebecca asked the shop assistant, "Do you have anything on the high exclusive list?"

"One moment, madam," the assistant said as she picked the phone up. Rebecca waited. "Yes, madam. Please follow me." Opening the door at the back of the shop where upon another room was revealed with high end designer garments that Summer had never heard of. Rebecca asked Summer what her favourite colour was.

Simon was now trying on shoes, Jonathan had asked for five pairs of every day casual shoes and three pairs of dress shoes which Jonathan made him try on every pair, Simon asked him why when a shoe is a shoe. All he got to his response was a cold look.

Summer was now trying on clothes that she thought she would never see, never mind actually trying them on, Rebecca had said to her because of the value of the dresses, it would be wise to only purchase three and to add the less expensive designer garments to her wardrobe, Summer thought less expensive.

"It would cost me two months' pay to buy just one dress." She never thought in a million years she would be here now but, nevertheless, she was finding it quite exhausting to say the least, it was very tiring, this made her think back to when somebody said to her in the local pub that they were extremely tired and exhausted after a shopping day and then remembered what she said to her, 'oh dear what a shame', or words to that effect. Simon was all but done, Jonathan had a word with the tailor he was planning to have all the items delivered to the set address and must be delivered on time. He then gave the tailor his card and bid him a good day.

Summer was handed a glass of champagne as she walked in to the other room. This one had shoes gracefully placed on pedestals around the room. Yet again, she was in her dream world two hours later Rebecca had placed the order for no less than 16 pairs of shoes. She smiled at Summer saying welcome to my pass time. They both smiled at each other as now they were all done as well, then Rebecca did as Jonathan did. She told them where to deliver to and to make sure it was going to be delivered on time and then left them her card as they both walked out of the shop. "Now let's go and get something to eat," she said as Charles opened the car door.

"Where to, madam?"

"I think the Roster would make a pleasant change." Charles closed the car door as he said, "The Roster it is." He then phoned Tony.

"They're going to the Roster A.T.A 1500 hours."

Simon asked him, “Are they ready now? We’ve been waiting here nearly one hour this is just like Summer.” Tony smiled at him through his rear-view mirror.

The Roster turned out to be a pub but all in all a very nice one the four of them sat down to a good old fashioned pub lunch which was right up Simon Street but not for Summer. A hour soon passed and the rest of the day was spent picking out luggage handbags and perfumes and aftershave, then they were finally back at the hotel and sat in Simon’s favourite bar. The one he was helped out of last night, Jonathan and Rebecca had done what they were asked to do and now said their farewells, the beer and wine was now sat on their table and with eager hands Simon brought his pint up to his lips to take a mouthful, he gasped.

“Now that’s good.”

Summer looked at him and smiled as she kicked her shoes off her now somewhat tied feet from under the table. “That was exhausting. I never thought buying clothes would make me so tired.” Simon turned to her with his pint pot still glued to his lips, he just nodded his head in agreement.

They had sat there for just over an hour, and Simon was four pints better off when Summer said, “Shall we go up to the room. It seems a shame to waste it as it’s our last night.”

Simon looked down at his beer and then at the bar and reluctantly agreed after all everything in the room was paid for as well, they made their way back to their room Summer with her shoes in her hand. On opening the door, the room was so inviting after the long day they both had just had but the beer fridge was now more attractive to Simon. Summer suggested having their evening meal on the balcony rather than dress and go down for dinner, to Simon this was nothing new as he nearly always had his meals in his room when he was away from home. Summer was the first to take a shower when the room door was knocked upon, Simon opened it with his bottle of beer still in his hand, two waiters stood there in the hallway both with food trolleys.

"Sir, your evening dinner." Simon looked over the first waiter's shoulder only to see the second waiter with a trolley as well.

"What has she ordered?"

The first waiter answered him, "Dinner for two, sir." Simon moved to one side as they both manoeuvred the trolleys through their room and on to the balcony. "Would sir prefer if we both stayed and serve?"

"No," Simon said as he put his hand in to his pocket, forgetting his place for a moment, the two waiters stepped back with embarrassment as Simon then said 'that will be all' as he pretended to be looking for his keys in his pocket.

A short time later, Summer came out of the bathroom, the thick towel bathrobe covered her body and as she pulled the shower cap from her head she said in her soft voice, "Your turn, and don't be long, I want to eat."

He thought to himself how romantic that was, NOT. Simon was in and out, dressed, and waiting for her within 15 minutes, she walked out of the bedroom and to say they weren't eating in the hotel restaurant, well she still looked stunning, Simon removed the lid from the first dish as Summer sat down he then served them both the first course.

A light breeze blew through the balcony doors as they sat there, the noise of the traffic below gave the whole experience a romantic feel. Summer started to weep as she sipped her red wine. She explained to Simon that she never thought she would ever get to do something like this.

"And after all, you've been through with the Fat Club and all the stress they put you through." She then took Simon's hand and thanked him.

Charles was heading home, no posh hotels for him, but nevertheless, he still had to be back mid-afternoon to take them both back to the train station, he was just coming out of the city when his phone rang, he answered it by saying,

"Charles."

"Hello, Charles." He knew the voice.

"Good evening, sir." He waited.

"Well, how did they do? Do you still think they're up to it?"

Charles began to explain, "Well, sir, whilst we all thought Simon was our man for the job, and don't get me wrong, sir, he still is, but Summer is the strongest of the two without her, I don't think he will pull this off." He explained that Jessica could see this from the first time they both walked into the hotel room. "And she didn't waste any time in telling them, but to my surprise, Summer actually retaliated and put Jessica into the corner, so sir, at the moment, everything is, and should, go to plan."

"Good. And Charles, please call me Teddy, as you know, we at the Fat Club don't stand on formalities, there will be times when you have to call me 'sir', but until then, it's Teddy. Now Charles, as you know I knew months before Jessica knew about her promotion, and that's why I moved you in to that sector first as you are well aware, and I can now tell you, you're now going to be Jessica's driver. Charles, in my business, it pays to keep once finger on the trigger, and

Charles, you're one of my many fingers. Is that understood?"

"Yes, sir."

"No, Charles."

"Sorry. Yes, Teddy."

"Good. I'll speak to you very soon."

Simon and Summer were enjoying the rest of their evening. The food was again to die for, in fact, everything was, they finished their evening with a glass of McCallum Lalique '62 for Simon and a glass of Magnum Cognac Grande for Summer, it was going to be their last night and what the hell, they weren't paying for it. The following morning soon came around. Simon turned over but to his surprise, Summer wasn't lying next to him, she was sat at the bedroom window. "Are you OK? Could you not sleep?"

"I want this life. I like this life," she said as she turned back to look out of the window. Simon could only rub her back to comfort her he then gave her a hug, he knew this was what Summer had always wished for but in his mind, it was better not to taste it, then to taste it and then not to be able to have it again. The time was now 11 o'clock in the morning. Two agents were now in their room ready to take them to yet another room. The four of them walked towards the lift then they stood there waiting as one of the agent's pushed the lift button, Simon noticed they were going up they were taking them up five floors, only the agents knew where they were going.

"Eighth floor," the soft voice of the lift's computer said as the door opened slowly giving the agent enough time to do a visual check of the hallway, he then moved is right hand up slightly, this was a sign for the second agent to stand fast, then giving the all clear. The door to the hotel room was literally opposite just a couple of doors down the hallway, one tap on the door that's all it was, just one tap they waited, as the door opened once they were all in the room Summer looked around straight away observing everything taking everything in, the room was the same as the others just dressed differently, they waited and then in she walked, again it was Jessica.

"Good morning." Summer looked down at her watch saying, just, in a sarcastic way.

Jessica took a deep breath saying, "Have you read your dossier?"

Summer held the dossier out at arm's length for her as Jessica somewhat awkwardly took it from her, Summer then sat before being asked as Simon followed her lead, Jessica took the floor and began her briefing, she waited for everybody's attention as if she was on centre stage waiting to start.

"You will both be picked up from your home by taxi, bring your suitcases, you don't have to put anything in them it's just for show, you will then be taken to a location where you will then take on the identity of Mr and Mrs Bay. From there, you will travel by limousine to the airport, and then fly first class to Rhodes, Charles will be driving you to the airport." He put his hand up to acknowledge them. "Once you're in Rhodes, you will be collected by a limousine and taken to the hotel."

Summer interrupted, "Is the driver of the limousine one of the Fat Club?"

Jessica answered in a patronising way, "No. Once you board the plane, you're on your own, but there will be a procedure to follow which I will discuss with you both at the end of the meeting, so if you have any questions, please keep them till the end and then will go over them." Simon looked at Summer and raised his eyebrows as if to say who does she think she is, Jessica continued to say, "Once in the limousine, you will be taken to the Dagmar hotel, where upon you will be then taken to your suite you must stay and, cannot stress this enough, you must now stay in character, you cannot use your own names from this point, not even in your own room as we don't know how secure your room is." Simon and Summer both nodded, Jessica once again was now walking around the room. Summer said to Simon, "I wish she would just stay in one place she's doing my head in," Simon agreed. "As Teddy has no doubt already told you both, you have to try and befriend Mr Slimm for this to work this is our chance to get to him, it may never happen again, in the dossier we left in your room for you both to read, did you both pay attention to page 11?" Simon and Summer looked at each other and then looked back at Jessica with a vacant look, Jessica had already pre-empted this reaction and had already prepared a copy of page 11 for both of them.

"Jacket cuff buttons." Once again, Jessica took control of the floor.

Summer thought to herself, How long is this going to go on for. She looked at Simon, noticing his eyes were becoming heavy so she placed her hand on his knee to bring him back around.

"This is the plan; we need you to get to Mr Slimm and, like I said, this is our last chance. Summer, you will be taking with you a small box, a sewing box to be precise, this will contain small cuff buttons in various colours these are specifically made for this purpose, they are designed with a location transmitter inside them and what we would like you to do is just sew one to his jacket."

Summer interrupted, "Oh, just as easy as that."

Jessica gave her a piercing look the kind of look that would turn someone to stone Jessica continued to say, "You both have two weeks to complete the task but you must stay the two weeks to avoid any detection, so what I'm saying is, if you complete it within the first week, you must, and I repeat, you must stay the rest of your holiday. Is that understood?" Once again, Simon and Summer nodded their heads. Jessica then carried on to say, "You will both fly out and back in to the United Kingdom on your own passports but when you get to your hotel in Rhodes you will use the passports identifying you both as Mr and Mrs Bay. They will be hidden in the lining of Summer's makeup case. You must put your original passports back it the lining for safe keeping. This is very important that you stick to this as we can guarantee that your room and all your belongings will be search by Mr Slimm's men." Simon looked a bit confused and concerned but more so for Summer. Summer, on the other hand, was taking it with a pinch of salt.

Things were now coming to a close; Simon's head was now becoming quite heavy and dropping from side to side with the tiredness, Summer had, on more than one occasion, tapped him to bring him out of it, all done and dusted. Jessica was now putting her paperwork back in to her briefcase as she reluctantly put her hand out to shake their hands, but to Jessica, this was not a sign of respect. Once again, the agents opened the door. The first agent looked up and down the hallway and then give the all clear to the second agent who then nodded to Jessica Green who made her exit once she was clear, the agent then said to Simon and Summer, "Please make your way to the lift and wait." Charles took the stairs to the next floor and then took the second lift.

They were now back in their room. One of the agents had explained to them that all the hush hush and secrecy had to be in place, so nothing was taking to chance. He then apologised saying again this is the reason for all the secrecy. Tea was now the order of the day, well at least for Summer as for Simon, well he already had a cup of coffee in his hand, everything had been a bit of a blur. Their three days had gone so quickly and their little adventure was now coming to an end but then an even bigger adventure was about to start, who knows what would be waiting for them only time would tell, but was time going to be on their side. Their bags were now packed and in the main lobby and the driver was waiting at the front door for them. Summer looked around for Charles. She had now taken a liking to him but only in a way that she felt safe when he was around her. The driver was now putting their luggage into the boot of his car as Summer took one last look around to see if Charles was there and to take the last look at the hotel as like the restaurant before it was something she would never experience again. The whole adventure was now as if it was on rewind, the drive back to the train station, then the journey by train from London to the midlands where Simon's car was parked, Summer was quick to get in, she sat there as Simon once again walked slowly around the car checking every panel his fingers softly moving across the paintwork as if he was caressing it, the weeks passed without a word from the Fat Club. Every morning, Summer would check for any emails, anything that would give her any news, but nothing came, her frustration was beginning to show, she would reluctantly put her NHS tunic on under the watchful eye of Simon as he knew she really wanted this now, she needed this excitement in her life she had now realised how boring her life really was, it was nothing to do with Simon as he was the love of her life, it was her work that was the problem, but the excitement wasn't to be, well not yet anyway. Another week passed and then it happened right out of the blue. Simon had it printed off ready for when Summer got home, the look on his face gave it away as soon as Summer walked in the house.

"It's on, isn't it?" He could see the look of relief on her face as she dropped her heavy bag in the hallway her eyes welling up. "When do we go?"

Simon handed her the print. "Off we go in six days, and Teddy says good luck."

Chapter 3

They were both standing at their living room window, waiting for the taxi to collect them, the time was now two in the morning and Summer wasn't best pleased, as she wasn't a morning person at the best of times, but then this was what the Fat Club wanted, and even though the flight wasn't till nine that morning, they still had to have their final briefing to go through before setting off for Rhodes.

"It's here," Simon said as the lights followed the crescent around to their house. Some of the bedroom curtains twitched from their neighbours. Simon always called this the curtain twitching ritual, but then this was something Summer would do as well.

She would often say to Simon, "I wonder where they're off to."

She would dream of faraway holiday destinations before getting back into bed, but now they were going on holiday, and this was a holiday with a difference. Their luggage was now packed away in the boot of the taxi still under the watchful eye of their neighbours. The driver asked them their names as Simon pulled the car door too.

"Mr and Mrs Rogers."

There was nothing on towards, but then the driver asked him a question, "Where was your last holiday?"

Summer took hold of Simon's hand as he replied, "Casablanca. Why do you ask?"

"Good," he said as he started the car. "My name is Short. I'm one of the drivers for the Fat Club."

Simon and Summer sat there, not knowing what to say next. They were now finally on their way, but to where? Unlike the service station before, this had to be some sort of hotel, but where? They had only been travelling 30 minutes or so when the taxi pulled into the small hotel car park, it was the sort of place business where people would stay overnight, Simon called it a one-night stop or low budget hotel but nevertheless, a pleasant one, the driver turned to them.

"We're here. Please leave your luggage in the boot and go directly to room three, where your contact is waiting for you both." Simon opened his door and then walked around to help Summer, now they were left standing as the driver pulled away.

Summer said, "Did you hear what his name was, Short, that's weird."

"You're right," Simon said as he looked around the carpark, "he must be at least six feet two."

They were now standing in the dark in complete silence with only a shimmer of light from the reception doors that led them the way in, once inside, they walked past the person on the desk who asked, "Have you had a good night, sir?"

Simon turned to him. "Yes, thank you." He then took Summer's hand and looked at her, in return he got a somewhat blank expression, the problem was, where was room 3, Simon couldn't really ask the person on the desk as that would no doubt give the game away as they were already supposed to be booked in but as luck would have it he seen a directional sign, rooms one to 10 with an arrow pointing the way, they finally got to the room after opening three fire doors along the way as Summer dragged her feet. Simon tapped on the door as not to wake anyone. He then heard the sound of the lock turning as the door open slightly, and the voice said, "Who is it?"

"Who do you think it is," Summer said, her patience was now wearing thin. Finally, they were in the room with Summer now sitting on the end of the bed worn out.

"Good morning. My name is Timothy. I'm here to greet you on behalf of Jessica Green."

Summer interrupted, "Hmmm, I wonder why she couldn't be here herself, a bit too early for her is it?"

Simon had to step in to calm things down.

Timothy was taken back by her sudden and unexpected manner, but he carried on to say, "This is your briefing." He then pointed to the small square table in the room where documents were laid out. "These are all your particulars, as you can see your flight details are here, you will be flying first class to Rhodes and, of course, on your return flight as well, here are your passports. Do you have your original passports with you?" Simon took them from his inside pocket and passed them to Timothy, he checked them and then gave them back, Simon looked at him as if to say, and Timothy explained how awkward would it be if your passport is out of date, he continue to say, "When you arrive at your destination, your passports must be hidden at all times." He picked up Summer's makeup case that was placed in the corner of the room and then placed it on the table in front of them. Once opened, he showed them the secret compartment. "This is where your original passports will be kept."

Simon asked him, "Why can't you just keep the passports for us, and we just fly out as Mr and Mrs Bay?"

"No," Timothy said, "in the unlikely event that something did go wrong, and I must stress that every avenue has been covered, but nevertheless in the event that something did then your fake passports should be disposed of and then revert back to your original passports and then make your way to the British embassy, is that clear?" Simon nodded once again in disbelief, he had done quite a bit of nodding throughout this escapade, whereas Summer once again just took it in her stride just sitting there on the end of the bed staring at the wall her eyes heavy, and every now and then saying, "Do you know this is the middle of the night." They both watched as Timothy put their fake passports into the makeup case. The next thing was to go over the money side of things, now Summer was awake, now she was back in the room her eyes were like pan lids, now she was showing some interest, Timothy continued, "There will be a credit card in your names, of course that will be Mr and Mrs Bay your credit limit on the card will be…" Summer waited "…£50,000." She bit her lip. "If, for any reason, you need cash then this is the card you must use, anything you buy over £500 must have a receipt. Is that clear?" Again, they both nodded, one hour had passed when Timothy then placed two small clear plastic bags on the table each had a white label with their names printed on them, "Please put all your personal belongings into your bags." Timothy then stepped back and waited. "Watches, money, jewellery, wallets, gold chains, everything." Or so they thought, but then Timothy asked them for their wedding rings.

Simon stepped forward. "Why do you need our wedding rings? What right do you have to ask for them?"

Timothy calmed him down. "This is why," he carried on to say, "in the unlikely event that you do need our help, there will be a telephone number you can contact us on this number will be inside the ring. Summer, we will need your engagement ring as well." Simon looked at him. "I know how you both must be feeling now, but we have to set the scene and it has to be just right for it to work." He then opened a small dark-blue box and inside was a four-carat diamond solitaire ring.

Summer, with no hesitation, put her ring into the bag, saying to Simon, "It's only for two weeks." Her eyes wide open.

"Right." He then gave them both their expensive watches and jewellery that had been bought for them when they were in London. Timothy then asked Simon and Summer to sign for them and in return, their small bags were put away for safe keeping.

"Just one more thing and you'll be on your way." He asked them to change into their new clothes that were hanging in the wardrobe for them, and he would give them 40 minutes to do so before calling back as at that time the car should be outside waiting for them, he then closed the door behind him.

They looked at each other just for a minute; Summer still sitting on the end of the bed, Simon wasn't happy about what was going on. Summer, on the other hand, was too busy looking at her ring.

"Look how it sparkles. What do you think, does it look good on my finger?"

Simon stopped her. "Summer, what are you doing? Didn't you hear what I just said?"

She turned to him with her no-nonsense response, "Simon, lighten up a little, we're going on holiday, let's just enjoy it for now and see what happens." They were both finally ready Summer took one last look in the mirror. She looked stunning in her sky blue knee length dress with a camel colour knee length coat and shoes to match all from a top designer, as she looked again at herself she said to Simon, "Maybe Rebecca does know what she's doing after all." She then turned to Simon, wow there he was in a suit that actually fitted him, he looked the part as well it's surprising how good you can look with the right money, it was now or never and Summer was now ready to go.

Timothy tapped on the door he complemented them both on how they looked then said it was time to get back down to business. "Right. Are we all ready to go? You have your passports, and you know as from when you get in your car at the other end you are Mr and Mrs Bay, stick to what you've been told and don't deviate, understood?"

They both said yes as Summer took a deep breath, then Simon said, "What about the man at the reception? He seen us both coming in."

Again, Timothy explained, "We booked a second room and, as we speak, one of our own men has him up in his room making a complaint, so you see, the reception area will be clear shall we go."

The car was waiting outside for them both, a black four wheel drive, to be exact, and from this moment on, it was going to be the high life with a very high lifestyle for the next two weeks. Summer was already playing the part. As they walked outside, she could see it was Charles waiting at the car Summer smiled.

"Good morning to you both, or should I say, A K A Mr and Mrs Bay. I'll be your driver for the journey to the airport." He smiled as he said it. They both sat back to enjoy the ride. There wasn't any traffic on the roads at that time in the morning and once there, they were then taken straight to the VIP lounge as Charles booked their luggage in, Simon had been in airport loungers before with Summer but this was something totally different, this was definitely 'only for the very wealthy'. There was champagne, caviar and canapés. With the help of two hostesses to help them with anything else, Summer wasn't hanging around she was in there helping herself to the champagne and canapés when one of the hostesses ask Simon if he would like something to drink, he quietly said he would like a beer if that was possible.

The hostess replied to his request, "That's not a problem, sir. I will get you a morning beer that I think will be to your taste." She then picked up the phone and within 10 minutes, one of the airport porters came into the lounge with four bottles of beer, the hostess then took it to one side and prepared one bottle, it was then placed in front of Simon ready for the tasting, she stood at a short distance eagerly waiting for his comments. The beer was wonderful it tasted of blueberries and cinnamon, weird, not in a million years would he have asked for a beer like this but Simon showed his approval, and with that said, the hostess then moved back to her position and waited, Simon turned to Summer, how the other half live.

One hour had past but it only seemed like they had just got there when the hostess got everybody's attention by saying, "Ladies and gentlemen, you will be asked to board in 20 minutes." Simon had just finished his second beer as the call was put out for first class to board, Summer still had a tight hold of her designer handbag it was something she never thought she would have, so even if it was only for two weeks, it was still something she was not going to let out of her sight, it was only a short walk to the boarding gate and they passed straight through, now sat in their seats they were feeling a little bit more relaxed, after all, it had already been a long day and now it was just starting.

One hour into the flight, and Summer was fast asleep with her headphones on, courtesy of the flight stewardess. Simon, on the other hand, was taking advantage of the free drinks after having the morning beers.

What the heck, he thought to himself. He was on the Bacardi and Coke. Every now and then, he would gaze out of the window he could see they were now flying over France.

"Would sir like to select from the menu?" Summer woke from her deep sleep taking her headphones off as she did so. "Dinner well be served in 30 minutes, sir, madam, can I get you drinks?" Summer was awake now and feeling better she looked at Simon her eyes still red with sleep.

"Where are we?"

"Somewhere over France, but not sure where though, it won't be long before we fly by Italy and then it's on to Rhodes." And what made it even better was they were next to be served. The stewardess placed their trays gently on their seat table that were fitted to their seats not like the pull-down tray tables that you got on a normal flight, it was so well presented with real napkins none of your paper rubbish and proper cutlery, none of your plastic knives and forks here, Summer took a sip of her chilled champagne and in doing so, she shivered.

"That's better," she said as she started with her first course. "Delicious," she said looking at Simon's food and then back at hers as not to be hard done by, 40 minutes later and they were now flying over the coast of Italy, the sea reflecting from the sunlight like a broken mirror that had been dropped onto the floor from some height, Simon took Summer's hand and squeezed it tight for reassurance. She looked at him with her knowing smile and quietly said, "We're going to be all right, don't worry." Simon smiled back at her even though it was a somewhat agitated one.

The coastline of Italy was now fading into the distance and a new coastline was now coming into view, it was the island of Rhodes, Simon started to tell Summer about Rhodes and Knights of St John and the Crusades but Summer was having none of it, she had better things to think about, things like having a good time and spending the Fat Club's money. The turquoise sea glistened as the plane started its descent to Rhodes Airport and as it moved to make its final descent the on-board speaker system alerted the cabin crew to their stations, Simon and Summer were now there on the island of Rhodes, the largest of Greece's Dodecanese islands, as the plane moved slowly to its resting place, Simon could see the luggage trucks following the plane from behind like ducklings following its mother as it finally came to its resting place. The fasten your seatbelt's light turned off just as the air steward walked down the first class aisle asking them to disembark, Summer stood up then realising she had no need to, as the stewardess would collect their overhead luggage, her makeup case was passed down to her and also Simon's jacket, the day ahead was going to be a hot one as you would expect for a place like Rhodes and being first class passengers, they were both quickly moved through the airport lounge along with the other privileged few. Once outside, away from the crowds of holiday makers that lined the waiting area for their coach transfers. They noticed a driver waiting holding a small broad up with Mr Bay written on it which in itself gave Simon a flashback to the days when he was Mr Bays driver, Simon made eye contact with the driver.

"Sir, are you Mr Bay?"

Simon answered him. "Yes. I take it you're my driver?"

"Yes, sir. I am here to take you to your hotel, please." His English was poor but understandable. He settled them both down in the back of the red hotel limousine and then collected their luggage from their luggage dolly. Their drive would last for 20 minutes along the narrow winding roads to the hotel a low volume of Greek music lightly entertained them on their way. They both had a sigh of relief as the car then turned the last corner to show off the long tree lined drive way which also had an abundance of pink hibiscus as the limousine made its way to the hotel. Two guards stood at the entrance, both wearing whiter than white uniforms and brandishing small firearms neatly tucked away, out of sight out of mind, this was only to keep the undesirables at bay, after all, this was a high class hotel, as the limousine pulled to a stop one of the guards asked for their names.

Simon leaned forward his window halfway down. "Mr and Mrs Bay."

The guard took his time going down the list until he came to their name. "Yes, you are correct."

Simon turned to Summer. "Is this some sort of game show?"

Summer couldn't help but laugh, he then ordered the other guard to open the gates and said as the car past through, "Welcome to the Dagmar Hotel."

"How the other half live," Simon said as they drove up to the front of the hotel again pink hibiscus complemented the white brick entrance. The grounds were like his local golf course, finely close cut grass but there were no signs here saying keep of the grass, sun loungers were placed near the pool but not to close, outside bars were also placed nearby and again it wasn't for the guests it was for the waiters. After all, you didn't get your own drinks in a place like this, the waiters got them for you, this was pure opulence. Their car slowly pulled around the large circular garden and then stopped at the side of the large sun canopy, two doormen eagerly awaited for their arrival dressed in Greek regalia. Summer waited for her door to be opened she was going to enjoy every moment of this. The warm air took her breath away as she stepped under the canopy and then in to the vast hotel foyer with Simon close behind her, vast was an understatement the floors were highly polished marble all handles were polished stainless steel. The lifts were situated in the corner of the main foyer with bell boys waiting to assist you. There was also a very large staircase that nobody could miss. It was as if it was made for a film in Hollywood which was strategically position at the other end of the foyer. Summer looked over and watched as a lady came down the right hand side of the stairs a bell boy followed closely behind his white gloved hand on the handrail wiping any smudges away and as he came down the bell boy on the left hand side climb the stairs to the top; again his white gloved hand did the same job. He then waited at the top as did the boy at the bottom of the stairs. Simon's attention was diverted to the main desk.

"Passports please."

Summer looked over his shoulder from behind him, becoming aware of the couple booking in in front of them.

"Passports please." Simon looked at Summer his eyes wide open a look of concern on his face.

"We still have our original passports on us," he said as he looked over to the main desk.

Summer picked up her makeup case and then calmly said to avoid any unwanted attention, "Give me the passports and wait here." She made her way to the restroom once inside she locked herself in to one of the many cubicles, but these were cubicles with a difference they were big enough to hold a washbasin, toilet and a chaise lounge.

"Would Madame like any assistance?" the restroom maid asked.

"No, I can manage, thank you," Summer said in her calm voice, she then listened to the maid's footsteps as she walked back to her chair at the entrance door. Summer muttered to herself. "Why didn't I see her when I came in, that could have been awkward, she must have been cleaning one of the cubicles." Summer put her makeup case on the dressing table and then unzipped the secret pocket, there they were, two passports, she took them out and placed them on the table she then put hers and Simon's original passports back into the secret compartment and zipped it back up then pushing the zip head in to place to conceal it. Now nobody could tell they were there. She then brushed her hair and then checked that she had the right passports before leaving the restroom. Simon was trying not to draw any attention to himself and there was a sigh of relief as he seen Summer walking back towards him, she smiled as she did so. She felt so alive her body tingling with excitement and as she got close to him she kissed him on the cheek as she slowly slipped the passports back in to his jacket pocket without anybody seeing. It was now time for them to book in after all it had been a long day and there bed was calling them, everything went well at the main desk as you would expected, what could have possibly gone wrong, room 19. Simon took the key card as the receptionist brought the palm of her hand down to the small bell on the desk in front of her and within seconds a bell boy was standing next to them.

"Room 19," the receptionist said in a stern voice and as they both turned to walk to the lift.

Simon said, "After the day we have had, maybe we'll do the stairs tomorrow." As they, walked they noticed their luggage was going the opposite way, it was off to the luggage lift, one would never have your luggage travelling with you in the lift at a hotel like this, it was unheard of.

The bell boy was there waiting for them as they arrived at their room. "May I, sir?" the boy said as he opened the door with their card. He then walked in front of them putting their luggage into the middle of their room and then quickly leaving as one of the security managers walked in.

"I am here to activate your safe."

"OK," Summer said, he walked her over to the discreetly hidden safe in the corner of the room and then asked if she was right or left-handed. Summer held her right hand out as he then asked if she would be so kind as to place her first finger of her right hand on a small square pad it gave a single bleep, the safe was now set.

He then explained, "To open and close your safe, you have to place your finger on the pad." He then did the same for Simon before walking around their room pointing out certain things of interest and then respectfully bowing to them and left, at last they were both now on their own, their room was enormous with moving partitions which made it as large or as intimate as they liked. Summer made a B line for the balcony; she slid open the large door to the side and stepped out in to the sunshine the patio itself was bigger than their patio and the front room put together back home. She then noticed another set of doors to the right of her. They led to their bedroom she then turned around from the overwhelming sea view to see Simon at the back of the room. He looked so far away, but his look was so worrying.

Summer had decided there and then that nothing would ever happen to him nobody would harm him, penny for them. Simon snapped out of it and smiled at her. "I'm just a bit tired that's all, after all, it has been a long day."

Summer wrapped her arms around him surrounding him with her love and reassuring him. "Come on," she said, "let's get out of these clothes and we'll get something to eat."

"What about having a sleep? That's what you said didn't you." Summer looked at him she was too excited to sleep now. She smiled as they unpacked and put everything in its place, and as they did they couldn't help but notice how big the room really was. There were many different areas for entertaining and of course relaxing to, and all of this with a pull or a push of a screen. Summer had decided on a long pink maxi dress with small dark blue flowers for herself and she was in the middle of laying out Simon's clothes as he walked in.

"You look fantastic," he said as he ran his hands down the side of her waistline. The fabric felt soft and cool to touch.

"Are you feeling better now?" she said as she carried on laying out his clothes.

"Yes, a little, I think it's with not having a lot of sleep."

Summer interrupted him. "I also think it could have been all the Bacardi and Cokes, don't you?"

"Maybe," he said as he got into the shower to bring himself around.

Summer was sitting on a relaxer on the balcony when Simon walked out. "You look so handsome." She had laid out a beige chino white shirt and beige shoes to match.

"Shall we go?"

"Yes," Summer said as she finished her champagne.

Summer had decided to take the stairs rather than the lift as it was all about being noticed now as that was part of the Fat Club's plan, they now had to introduce themselves as Mr and Mrs Bay, Summer walked down the stairs as if she had just been told she had won an Oscar with the bell boy closely behind her wiping any marks away from the stainless steel handrail, there walk down had done the trick it had got them noticed.

Summer whispered, "It's as if we're being vetted by the other guest's, you know, when you walk it to a room and everyone stops and looks you up and down." Summer then laughed out loud as if Simon was flirting with her and then said, "That will get them talking about us, don't you think?" Simon looked at her in a puzzled way. Summer again turned to him saying, "You have a lot to learn." As they both got to the bottom of the stairs.

"Sir, madam, can I help you in any way?" The head porter stood there and waited for their reply.

"What would you like, dear?" Simon said, now knowing the game was on, he was now getting into character, most definitely playing Mr Bay.

"What would you like, my dear? Sea food would be nice I think, yes sea food and champagne."

Simon looked at the head porter. "I think a table for two in a nice quiet spot that's what we'll go for." He then turned to Summer and smiled.

For the next three days, things were the same. They were having such a good time, which, in Summer's eyes, was needed and of course, they had made themselves noticed, to the point where a lot of the guests wanted to be with them, they were living the high life in every way. In the mornings, they were visiting landmarks around the Island, and of course, they were chauffeur-driven, and then in the evening, eating at one of the many restaurants on the resort, this was the part Summer loved the most as she would often dress to kill. And then on Thursday afternoon, as they were both sunbathing at the pool near to reception it all changed, they noticed four men nearby waiting to check in keeping their luggage close to them. Simon had noticed there was no flight labels on their cases.

Summer said, "That's strange."

Simon turned on to his front and said to Summer, "It looks like they may have come by boat."

Summer looked at him and said nothing. "Back in a minute," Summer said as she got up and walked over to reception, Simon trying to grab her top inconspicuously to stop her.

"Yes, madam. How may I help you?"

Summer stood next to one of the four men. "No please, deal with these gentlemen first."

One of the men then turned to her. "You're so kind," he said in an American accent. He then asked, "How long have you been here?"

"Four days now. It's a lovely place."

"Right," he said in his deep American voice, he then introduced himself as Bailey, "And yours?"

She nearly said 'summer' and if she had, then the game would have been over before it had even started. "Juliet. I'm here with my husband; there he is at the pool," Summer pointed. Just as Simon looked over, she waved as Simon waved back. Unintentionally, she had made herself look a little giddy, which wasn't really a bad thing in view of what was about to happen.

Bailey asked her, "Where's the best places to go in the hotel?"

She was quick to recommend one of the bars, she continued to say, "As it happens, my husband and I will be visiting that bar this evening, we may even bump into you later." Then as Summer walked back towards Simon, he couldn't help but notice how the four men were looking at her. Simon turned back over on to his back as Summer lay on her sun lounger.

"Well," he said, "is it them?"

"Without a doubt," Summer said as she put her sunglasses on and then lying back and watch them discreetly as they walk through the grounds to the chalet blocks there going towards the orange block. The chalets were still up market but just not on the same par with the hotel. "We'll have to get their chalet number to see what's going on." They then both watched as the four of them turned the corner out of their sight. The day was unbearably hot as they lay there. To the other guests, they looked the perfect couple with not a care in the world, well, they were the perfect couple, but as for not have a care in the world, well, if only they knew what was going to happen next. Simon put his hand up to get the attention of a pool side waiter and within seconds he was standing over him.

"May I help, sir?"

"Yes please, would it be possible to have some cold melon?"

"Is that for two, sir?" Simon looked across to Summer. "Yes for two."

The melon came on a silver platter, anywhere else it would have been on a plastic plate but not here, like Simon had said 'pure decadence', each individual piece of melon was cut the same as the rest and a small cocktail stick placed in the centre of each piece at the same height as the rest. Simon said to Summer, "It's a shame to spoil it, but waste not want not."

The evening was still young, and they had now returned to their room. Simon was sat on the balcony with a tall glass of chilled beer from their refrigerator next to their drinks cabinet. His coffee was redundant for the time being, he was already itching to get to the bar and restaurant. On the other hand, Summer yet again was in and out of the bathroom. "What do you think of this, Simon?"

"You look fantastic."

"Do you think so?" Summer said as she put something else on. "What about this then?"

"My God, that's gorgeous."

Summer looked at him. "Am I boring you?"

Simon put his glass down on the table and turned to her. "Summer, you look lovely tonight, and you are never boring but let's be honest, it's getting late and we do need to make a move."

"Yes," she said. "Yes, you're right, this will have to do."

He looked at her saying, "This will have to do? You're wearing a £1500 dress." But then this was something Summer always said even at home. Simon always said it was her catchphrase, 'this will have to do', even though she had been at it for two hours. They walked down the main stairs and on to the main lobby and yes, they stole the show again. Well, Summer did in her black knee length dress with an open back, gold necklace with a single diamond a matching bracelet and a small black shoulder bag designer, of course, her shoes were the finishing touch. As for Simon, he had one of his designer dinner suits in dark navy with shoes to match and a whiter than white shirt to finish it off, open neck of course. As they finally got to the lobby, they were met by their crowd of friends they made acquaintance with whilst at the hotel. Summer looked over to the main doorway to the bar area, through the doorway she could see the four men standing at the bar.

She whispered in Simon's ear, "They're at the bar, follow me in." In five minutes, Summer then turned to the ladies of her group. "Come on, girls, let's have a drink." Simon kept the men back for a moment or two, her plan had come together just as Simon walked into the bar the four men had introduced themselves to Summer and the group of ladies.

"Just in time, darling," Summer said. "This is my husband."

Simon held his hand out, but he had no takers they said hi but none of them took his hand.

"So, where are you going from here?" Summer asked.

Bailey replied in his deep American accent, "We're going into the town. Going to hit some bars, see what's going on."

"Going on?" Summer said, with Simon being drawn into the conversation Bailey carried on to say, "You know how it goes." Bailey now had his spectators, he was now as he would say 'in the main field' but was soon played out by one of his own colleagues, stopped by a hand on his shoulder. Bailey looked around heavy with drink, they were now eye to eye. Nobody moved and then Bailey smiled. "Come on, guys, let's get out of here and grab some beers." His colleague took his hand off Bailey's shoulder and smiled with him as all four walked out of the bar.

Summer turned to Simon. "We now know his calcaneal."

"And that is?" Simon said as he placed his glass on the bar.

Summer took a sip of her champagne. "It's the drink."

"You mean his Achilles heel." Summer just looked at him.

The night was drawing to a close and a fantastic time was had by all but they both knew the holiday was really over for them and the whole thing would be ending soon.

"We need to get some information about when Mr Slimm is going to be having these meetings."

Simon agreed with her, but his concerns were not knowing when he was going to be using the hotel, what three days or nights was he actually using the hotel.

"Yes," Simon said, "but what three?"

Summer then said, "We could have some drinks with Bailey, if we can just get him on his own then I can maybe get his room card and have a look around whilst you keep him occupied."

"And how are we going to do that? Let's be honest, we don't even know if they're all in the same room."

Summer looked at him. "Are you kidding me? Have you seen them? They would have killed each other by now if they were all in the same room."

"Maybe," Simon said. "Well go on then, how do you suggest we go about it?"

"We bump into him at breakfast. That's the best time because that's when he's on his own. We tell him we're having drinks in the evening with some friends and then invite him and only him. We can make some excuse as to why the other three cannot attend. We could say our guests felt intimidated by them."

Simon finished his drink. "Do you think he will go for it? We're going to be taking a big chance on this."

Summer picked up her glass, it was empty. "Trust me, his ego will overcome him. He will be there; we just need to set it up. Now get the drinks in."

Chapter 4

The day after the night before. And how many times had Simon been told that, especially from his beloved wife Summer. Well this again was the morning of the night before and yes Summer was sat on the end of their bed saying exactly that, she told him she had been up most of the night thinking how they were going to get around it; the plan was plain and simple.

"We get to him at breakfast. After all, he's an American, and Americans eat, well especially at breakfast. Right, then with that in mind, we're going to be having breakfast on the terrace this morning."

Simon rolled over pulling the bed sheets over him as he did so saying, "No please, just let me sleep a little longer." The breeze was blowing in from the sea that morning. Simon could hear the trees rustling in the light wind, and if there was a volume button, he would have turned it down a little. Summer was going to have her fruit and yoghurt and Simon was having his cereal with of course his two painkillers on a small plate next to it. The scrambled egg came afterwards but only if he was up to it. They both got to the terrace one hour late surely Bailey hadn't been and gone they waited in anticipation and their waiting paid off Simon's extra hour in bed even though they didn't know it at the time had done the trick. In he walked and what was even better he was on his own. Summer got hold of Simon and pulled him from his chair his painkillers in his hand now pulling him quickly around the back of the terrace to a small pathway that would lead them both down to the beach, once there they had a five minute walk back around to the front of the hotel, they then stood in the lobby catching their breath before walking back in to the breakfast room, where the waiter looked twice at them with a somewhat bewildered look as he was convinced they were out on the terrace.

"Just coffee, please," Summer said making herself heard, she now had his attention. "Good morning, Bailey. How was your night?"

"Heavy," he said as he ordered pancakes. "Yours?" he said in an abrupt way.

"Quiet," she said. "May we join you?"

He pointed to the chair as he took a sip of his freshly squeezed orange juice, it wasn't long before Bailey asked, "So, what are you both doing tonight?"

Summer could not believe what he had just said it was all going her way, and she thought this was going to be hard. "We're having drinks with friends tonight in the southern bar. Have you been there? You're welcome to join us." Bailey poured maple syrup all over his pancakes to the point where it started to run off the sides of his plate.

"I'll have a word with the rest of the crew and get back to you."

Summer put her coffee down on to the table. "There's a problem with that," she said as she slowly stirred her coffee looking at Simon. "As my husband will agree, won't you, darling? The people were meeting up with tonight like your company but your company only, they don't really care for your friends, in fact, dare I say this but they find them quite repulsive."

Simon looked at Summer had she taken this a bit too far, he then looked back at Bailey saying, "Yes I quite agree, sweetheart." And then waited for Bailey's reply.

He laughed out loud his ego had grown even more now. "Yes, you're right. They do go a bit over the top."

Summer thought to herself, A bit over the top that was an understatement.

Another spoonful of pancakes was guided into his mouth as the maple syrup ran down his chin, he said, "So it's in the southern bar at what time?" They now had him his own ego had won him over yet again.

"7:30," Summer said still slowly stirring her coffee.

"That's a bit early, isn't it? It's only because some of our friends would like to meet you before they go out for the evening, but if you can't make it then we both would understand."

"No, no its OK. I'll be there. See you later then."

That was their queue to get up and leave. Once outside away from anyone who could be listening in on them, Simon said, "Why on earth did you say the southern bar?"

There was a reason behind Summer's madness, and she explained, "First of all, look how close Bailey's chalet is to the southern bar, go on how far away from the bar would you say it is?"

Simon looked. "Maybe five minutes or so."

"And how far is our room from the southern bar?"

Simon looked at her. "Fifteen minutes or so."

She then looked back at him with open eyes. "And?"

"Just stop beating around the bush Summer and just tell me how we are going to do it."

She began, "You're going to spill a drink down my lovely top and of course, I'll be so upset with you."

"Right," Simon said looking a bit puzzled.

"So I'll have to go back to our room to change which is…" She looked at Simon and waited, again there was an air of silence.

"Right," he said, but still not getting it.

Summer sat him down and explained how it would work. "We meet him in the bar and get some drinks down him, that's the most important thing we need to do. We then tell him our friends couldn't make it after all but by that time he'll be so far gone with drink and won't be that bothered anyway, you will then spill a drink over me and I will then have to go to our room to change, but little will he know that there'll be one of my tops in a bag behind the tree's just outside the bar, that will give me a good 30 minutes to get in his chalet and get the meeting dates and times."

Simon asked the question, "OK, how are you going to get into his chalet?"

"With his card key, of course."

"And how do we get that?" he said.

"WE don't," Summer replied, "YOU do, first of all we need to know what pocket his key card is in and then we get him to the toilet and that's where you come in." Simon put his head in to his hands and let out an almighty cry, Summer reassured him, "It will work, trust me." Simon spent the rest of his day in their room nursing his hangover as for Summer well she was out on the sun loungers again. She asked Simon if he wanted her to stay with him but all he wanted was to sleep it off. No sooner had his head hit the pillow and closed his tired eyes, he felt a gentle tap on his shoulder and the smell of sun lotion and burnt skin with a faint smell of perfume woke him from his sleep. It was a strange combination but nevertheless a somewhat pleasant one. Summer slowly brought him around. "How are you feeling now?" "Better," he said.

"You'll feel even better after a shower and something to eat and maybe a couple of pints, you know, the hair of the dog." Summer looked stunning absolutely gorgeous in yet another one of her many outfits purchased by the Fat Club and they were both now sat at the table in the southern bar, sat waiting with one eye on the door when in walked Bailey, the drinks started to flow as did Bailey's ego. Summer then explained that her guests couldn't make it and that they felt awful that they'd ruined his evening but he was welcome to stay and have some drinks with them, Bailey agreed, yet again the plan was going Summer's way, more drinks were consumed when she said she had something in her eye blinking and then again as she looked for her compact mirror in her bag as she did so she put her key card on the table as she put the compact up to her eye saying, "I often thought how do these key cards work because they all look the same." Bailey jumped in straight away. "It's the bar code." "Bar code," Summer said.

"How do you mean?" Simon just could not believe what was happening, he couldn't believe how Summer was playing him and more to the point was this how she played him back home.

"Bar code," Summer said again.

“Yes,” Bailey said as he reached for his breast pocket, and with two fingers he pulled out his key card putting it on the table in front of him, he then began to tell them how it works, and they both tried to look interested while he waffled on before putting it back in to the same place, more drinks where consumed, doubles for Bailey without him knowing and eventually there was a call of nature. Simon pressed his foot down hard on to the leg of Bailey’s chair causing him to stumble. He then quickly caught him before he hit the floor.

“Are you OK? I think you need to get to the men’s restroom, come on I’ll go with you.” Simon smiled at Summer as he did so. After some delicate manoeuvring past the tables in the bar, they eventually got to the restroom. He held Bailey up against the wall as he was now a little worse for wear Simon then got his attention. “I think it best if you use the cubicle rather than drawing attention to yourself.” Bailey agreed, Simon then asked to take his jacket and once he was in the cubicle Simon closed the door. He heard the lock slip across. This was his chance to get the key card from his pocket and as he did so he checked around the rest room. All was OK they were on their own. He then picked up a napkin from one of the wash basins wrapping the key card up in to it and then waited for Bailey to finish, after a long delay, the door open.

Bailey stood there Simon asked if he was OK to which Bailey replied, “I’ve been better.” Eventually, they both made it back to their table. Simon apologising to people along the way, but he did smile a little thinking to himself, where’s your ego now. At last, they were sat at their table Simon nodded to Summer and then knocked his drink down her top she quickly stood up.

"Darling, what have you done to me?" People in the bar looked around as to all the commotion as Simon could only apologise as he gave Summer the napkin and then taking her hand pressing it against the key card, she acknowledged him by putting her hand on his Summer apologised to Bailey for the inconvenience and asked him to stay while she got changed. He muttered something to her that only he could understand as she turned to Simon. "Keep a close eye on him." He knew what she meant.

Summer was now outside the bar and had picked up the bag that was hidden behind one of the trees her heart was now racing, racing with excitement as she made it to Bailey's chalet well within the five minutes and was outside having a look around before committing herself to going inside; it was now or never. She took the card and slid it down the machine the luminous light changed from red to green as the door lock clicked open, she then cautiously pushed the door open asking, "Is there anybody home?" Silence, Summer asked again before going inside, a deep breath and another beeper breath was taken as she closed the door behind her, first thing first was to get out of her now sticky wet top, replacing it and then putting the soiled one back in to her bag leaving it close to the front door. Looking at her watch, Summer now had 20 minutes or so to get out and back to the bar. So where would the safe be thinking about it logically. The possibility would be that they're all in the same place within the rooms and Summer was right she walked straight to it but didn't anticipate what she was going to see next, yes it was a fingertip pad lock it had completely slipped her mind. Summer said out loud, "Come on, think about it what would you do." Looking at her own finger and then remembered a film her and Simon had seen. OK, what the hell, she started looking around the rooms as time was now of the essence she was soon in the last room, the bathroom and there it was, a glass on the shelf, Bailey's glass. She opened the bathroom cabinet to reveal a pack of wet wipes carefully putting them down next to the glass Summer now looked at where the first finger on the glass already knowing that Bailey was right handed. The next thing, she took the dark eyeshadow powder case from her bag and with her small makeup brush she dusted that part of the glass once that was done she then picked up the wet wipes and peeled off the self-sealing tab from the top, good it was still sticky. Summer now carefully placed the sticky tab on to the glass over Bailey's fingerprint and gently put pressure on to it and then very slowly and anxiously peeled the tab away from the glass she held her breath. His fingerprint was now on the wet wipe tab she wanted to check her time but thought better of it as not to put more pressure on herself, carefully walking over to the safe not wanting to drop the tab she then placed it gently on the finger pad then put her own finger on top of it, nothing happened, how can that be. She stood back from the safe and thought about it looking at her own finger, maybe just maybe, she rubbed her finger up and down the side of her leg causing static and then placed her finger back on the pad, a second time and to her amazement it worked.

The safe was now open. Summer now moved the contents of the safe remembering the way it was placed before doing so. Amongst the jewellery and passports, Summer found what she was looking for, two pieces of paper with dates and times, placing them on the table she took pictures of them from her phone before placing them back as she found them then double checking it was locked. She was now back in his bathroom wiping his glass and then put the sticky tab back onto the wet wipes. Everything was as it should be as she picked up her bag at the door but then Summer stopped for a moment turning around and taking a deep breath. She smelt her own wrist her perfume; it was that unusual it would give the game away. Putting the bag down, Summer went back in to the bathroom picking up Bailey's aftershave and spraying it around the chalet she then opened the front door checking outside before heavily spraying the door handle, this would put the scent of his own aftershave on to his hands she then placed the aftershave back in to his bathroom making sure it was as she found it just before leaving the chalet, it was done, she placed the bag back behind the tree and then walked back in to the southern bar.

"Hi, I'm back all clean now," she said as she sat down.

Simon's looks were a sign of great relief. "Are you OK now, dear?"

Summer looked at him and smiled. "Yes, darling, all done now."

Bailey interrupted the conversation, "You people, so typically British, so over-the-top with your pleasantries, it was a drink down your top for God sakes." He was now becoming quite argumentative because of the drink, Simon moved his finger around in a rotating manner so Summer could see he was indicating that it was time to speed things up a little and get the hell out of there she agreed, by now Bailey was slumped on the table Summer slipped his key card back in to his top pocket and then called the bar manager over, she then explained that he's had a little bit too much to drink and would it be possible for somebody to get him back to his chalet, they were only too happy to help. The evening was now quite pleasant as they both walked along the path of the hotel.

Simon asked how it went to which Summer replied, "It's a good job we watched all those spy movies in the past."

Simon then said, "What the hell is that aftershave?"

She stopped him. "Tell me something I don't know. I know it's bad and a very long shower will put it right anyway how did it go with Bailey when I left?"

Simon shook his head. "You have no idea. The man is an utter lunatic. Do you know he's killed people. I said to him 'that's a nice ring', I was just making light conversation but then he told me how he came across it."

Summer was hooked. "Go on."

"He told me he was in a bar somewhere in Brazil when this man walked in he noticed the ring he was wearing and Bailey asked him for it, you know Bailey being Bailey and all, the man laughed at him, so Bailey took it from him, finger and all, the man's an utter lunatic and certainly not to be crossed."

Summer said, "We're not here to cross anybody we're here to get this done and get home." She was now realising it wasn't going to be as easy as she thought it would.

Simon said just three words, "YOU don't SAY."

Now in the safety of their room, or as safe as their room could be, Simon sat on the balcony having a nightcap whilst summer was in the shower, washing away Bailey's dodgy aftershave eventually she sat down next to Simon with a tall glass of red wine. She thought she would never say this but she was sick of the sight of champagne.

"Right then, let's have a look at these pictures on my phone. There were two of them the first were times and meetings, the first meeting was going to take place the day after tomorrow at midday, it says they have the small, majestic function room."

"Yes, we've seen that," Simon said, "it's through the woodlands to the beach, that's going to be hard to reach him if he's in there. Where are the other meetings being held?"

Summer took a sip of her wine. "The second is in the veto bar."

"That's more like it, it's just off the main lobby."

They both acted like children as they high-five each other and finished their drinks just sitting there looking up at the stars. The following morning soon arrived. Simon woke up to find himself still on the balcony. Summer had decided it best to let him sleep. He pushed back the top sheet that Summer had put over him. He could hear ground workers going about their business laughing and joking about, obviously happy in their work, but for Simon and Summer, their time was now nearly at an end. They only had a just under a week left on the island. Simon slowly opened the sliding doors to find Summer sat up in bed. He asked if she was OK; it wasn't like her as he knew she liked her sleep. He sat on the end of the bed looking at her.

"What's going through your head; this isn't like you at all."

Summer pushed her back in to the pillows. "I've been thinking. Well truth be known, I been thinking for most of the night that's why I left you out on the balcony."

"So, what's on your mind?"

"Well, I now know it's going to have to be the veto bar."
"Yes," Simon said, "we said that last night."

"Yes, we did," Summer said as she took hold of his hand to shut him up so she could explain. "As I said it, we'll have to be the veto bar but we really need to be invited to his table. We're not going to be able to just walk up to him, are we? We both know that's not going to happen."

Simon made two cups of coffee and sat back down on the bed next to her. "Go on then, what have you come up with?"

"Well, we know Bailey and he knows us now, so if he's with Mr Slimm and we get Bailey to acknowledge us then with a bit of luck Mr Slimm will as well."

"What are you going to do, Summer? I don't like this."

"Trust me, he will notice us." Now she brought up the second picture the picture Simon didn't see last night. The information on this document worried Summer and it was about to make Simon anxious. She began to show him what she had taken. The document contained the names of the people Mr Slimm was meeting. "Day number one four, people are Mr McBride, Mr Dubois, Mr Akins and Mr Brouge. All four had large sums of money next to their names but look what it says next to Mr Brouge." Simon asked Summer to read it out to him, "It said, 'after the meeting take all four back to their hotels', but next to Mr Brouge, the instructions were for him not to reach the hotel." Simon looked at Summer. They both then looked back at the document. "It looks like the four are from the UK and the Channel Islands," Summer read down the document. "He's meeting another four the day after he's then staying at the hotel in the penthouse suite and seeing another five the following morning."

Simon had become fully aware who these people were, and he explained to Summer. "When I drove for Mr Bay, he was moved up the ladder so to speak, so these names we are looking at now are the next step up the ladder from Mr Bay, I've got it now these 13 people are Mr Slimm's generals."

The morning was yet again a pleasant one they both walked through the main lobby to the breakfast restaurant when they came across Bailey walking towards them, Simon said in a low voice as not to be heard.

"He doesn't look very happy."

"It looks like he's been in some sort of fight look at his eyes, they're all swollen."

Simon asked, "You didn't leave anything in his room, did you?"

"No," Summer said. "Well, I don't think I did." They stopped and waited for his response, Bailey stopped right in front of them Summer took Simon's hand and then looked at Bailey.

"What happened to you?" Simon said as Bailey rubbed his eyes.

"You didn't give me any sea food last night, did you?"

Simon knew straight away he was allergic to seafood. "No," he said. "You didn't eat the whole time we were with you."

Bailey apologised for his behaviour last night, his throat and mouth still tingling. Summer asked if he got to his chalet OK.

"Yes, I did. But don't know how the hell I got there."

Simon explained, "We had to get the bar staff to take you back."

Bailey could only thank them both as he carried on to reception. Summer held Simon back for a moment to hear Bailey say at the reception desk. "Have you made arrangements for Mr Slimm's arrival? Good, he should be here for midday."

Summer turned. "Did you hear that? It's midday, we need to be around the reception area when he arrives so we can get a look at him."

The order of the day was to do some chilling out or as Summer would say RT—relaxing time, not that the whole holiday was a big chill out for them. They really weren't in the mood for any more sunbathing; it was beginning to lose its zing plus they had more things to think about now, so people watching it was. They just sat there under the shade of the trees and watched the world go by. Summer had spotted Bailey walking around the main lobby near the reception desk she tapped Simon who was nodding off in the heat. "It's happening, he's here." Simon sat upright at their table with his Sunglasses on, both their heads turned away from the reception area, but their eyes stayed fixed on Bailey without making it too obvious.

Simon picked up his drink from the table. "I think this is him, what do you think?"

Summer turned to the side making it look as if she was getting something from her bag. "You're right, it could be him." She then turned back looking towards the pool while whilst Simon carried on watching him, he noticed he was quite rounded and about five foot four and from what he could see. His complexion was quite poor. He had very short black hair and a goatee beard with no moustache. Simon then turned back to look at the pool just for a couple of seconds trying not to look suspicious and then turned back to look at him one last time and as he did, so Summer whispered, "He looks a right sleaze ball."

Once Mr Slimm and his entourage had left the main lobby, Summer got up from her chair and walked through the lobby to reception.

"Good afternoon."

The receptionist looked up at her. "Good afternoon, Mrs Bay. How may I help?"

"I've noticed a function room called 'the Majestic' and would like to know if I can reserve it for the evening."

The receptionist replied, "It's booked already for this evening, can I ask what you were thinking of doing?"

Summer then sat down opposite to her. "I was thinking of throwing a cocktail party for some of my guests." Summer then turned the monitor on the desk slightly towards her, straight away she noticed Mr Slimm had a 7 o'clock booking. She then asked for a table for the following evening in the veto bar keeping hold of the monitor as she did so.

"What time would Madame like?" Summer quickly looked down the booking register, and there he was he had two tables book one for five people and one table for three. So, with that in mind, Summer booked a table for her and Simon for the same time. She finely got back to where Simon was. They finished their drinks then made their way back to their room to go over their plans.

"There's one thing that is worrying me, it's tapping away in the back of my head."

Simon asked what it was.

"Well, Mr Bay is in prison, yes?"

"Well, of course he is, what's your point, Summer?" "Again," she said, "well the four people Mr Slimm is meeting this evening are from England and if I'm going to get him to notice me as Mrs Bay…"

Simon stopped her. "My God, I didn't think of that. If one of them knew me by name." He looked at Summer.

"Right," she said. "Tonight, we have to conveniently bump into Mr Slimm in the main lobby on this way to the majestic room; we can't afford any slip ups, not when we're this close. Tomorrow we will conveniently leave the safe open that's just in case they come looking." Simon disagreed with this only because of the amount of jewellery that would be on display, after all it wasn't theirs; it belonged to the Fat Club he thought it would be better if Summer did it his way.

"And what way would that be?" Summer said as she poured a glass of wine for them both as Simon began to explain.

"The hotel has a car hire."

"Yes, they do."

"So why not get the information from reception as if we're going to hire a car then we could leave the information out on the table with the passports. I think that would be more convincing than leaving the safe open."

For once, Summer had to agree with him, for once he was right. Summer decided to go all out that evening, she put one of her top designer dresses on to the bed with accessories to match as always, she had to get noticed for this to work she then put Simon's clothes on the bed beside hers before going into the shower room. Simon sat on the balcony for 10 minutes or so just thinking things through, for him the holiday was over as he was now more concerned about what could go wrong. In the beginning, he was concerned about Summer not being up to the job but now he was worried about letting her down. He was now realising he was becoming the liability. He was the one who should be responsible for her not the other way around.

"Are you OK out there?"

He turned to see Summer dripping in her bath robe, her hair wet. "Yes, just finishing my drink."

She smiled at him saying, "Come on, your turn, the last one in always wipes down."

Their night out was going to be a restaurant in Rhodes old town; it was going to be their last meal together on the island. Their idea was to conveniently bump into Mr Slimm on their way out of the hotel. The game was now on. They were in the bar just off the main lobby in Summer's eyes. It was the best place to be as you could easily see who was coming in and out of the lobby from where they were sitting. They waited anxiously, and eventually there he was, he looked like a eighty's throwback movie star, his shirt was opened three buttons down and even though his hair was short he still had hair gel on, it looked like he had just dipped his head in a chip pan, Summer put him in his late 40s Bailey was there with him and another three men but there was another lady with Mr Slimm this time, she looked like she was some sort of personal bodyguard, it was now or never. Summer put her glass down on the table and walked towards Bailey. Simon was close behind her.

"Hi, what are you doing this evening?" It was her aim to come across all innocent. Mr Slimm's female bodyguard stood in front of him shielding his body with hers as she glared at Summer. Bailey awkwardly said hello.

Summer asked, ‘what are you doing tonight’ only to get a response of ‘I can’t really talk now’.

She noticed Mr Slimm looking her up and down. What a repulsive little man he is, she thought but the job had to be done and she now had the response she was looking for.

Simon then stepped in. “We’re off to Rhodes old town for the evening, maybe we’ll see you in the bar later on.”

Chapter 5

Summer looked back as she walked away, Mr Slimm was still looking at her, he was like a little fish on a line, something you would throw back into the water if you caught it, and Summer was the one who was about to reel him in. The bell boy opened the main lobby doors as Simon and Summer walked out on to the forecourt where a line of taxis waited, they could have taken the hotel limousine, but that evening was their last chance to have some time on their own and tonight was just for the two of them.

"Where to, sir?"

"The Helios restaurant in Rhodes old town please."

Once on their way, Simon looked at Summer and smiled and was just about to say something when he noticed the taxi driver looking at them through his rear-view mirror, Simon's mind was now all over the place playing tricks with him, and to be honest he didn't trust anybody now, for all he knew the driver could just be looking at his beautiful wife, or was he…

They soon arrived at the Helios restaurant. Again this was a place to be seen in. The restaurant itself was set on the front of the harbour its lights setting the scene as they shimmered into the water of the harbour bay and as they both entered they couldn't help but notice the fine Greek antique furniture.

Again this was a place that Summer knew she would never get to see again, this was a place she would only walked by looking in from the outside. They talked for most of the evening; it was all about home and of course Simon's work, he couldn't wait to get back to his business, but Summer she had now been put on this pedestal and she knew it was going to be hard to come back down.

"I love my job, but I need a bit more it's become lacking in interest and it's no longer exciting. I need more after this." Simon looked at her in astonishment taking her hand. What else could he do, all in all they had an excellent evening as there was no pressure on them to impress others, they walked for a little while as the Heavenly stars set the scene and yes just for a moment, they were Mr and Mrs Rogers again but now it was time to get back to the job in hand. Simon hailed a taxicab and they made their way back to the hotel where Summer decided to call it a night to the delight of Simon. She had a quick look in the bar on the way to their room. He was there waiting. Mr Slimm had definitely taken the bait he was sat there waiting with his minders. The following morning, Simon and Summer were sitting on their balcony when they noticed Bailey on the patio below them just outside the main doors. He was talking to the other three men which looked somewhat heated, but they couldn't really hear what was being said.

"No, he has to be the last. We have to get the other three back to their hotels first."

"What's the plan then?"

"We kill him by injection. It's quiet and not messy."

"Then what?"

Bailey continued to say, "We take the body out to sea in the Cruiser and then feed him to the fish."

They all started to laugh. "Lucky man, he's going to be fish bait."

"You can't double cross Mr Slimm and then think you're going to get away with it."

They all laughed again. Simon turned to Summer. "Bailey must have said something really funny because they're all laughing. I didn't think he had it in him." Summer had decided to start her packing early, she thought it best rather than leave it till the last minute and as she had said before the holiday was coming to an end anyway so there was no point in dwelling over it. Her case was placed carefully onto the room luggage rack in the corner and each item of clothing was caressed by her as she put it away. It was as if she was never going to see them again. They decided to stay in the room that day. The order of the day was to sunbathing on the balcony. To be honest, they were a bit worn out it had taking its toll and of course they were both thinking about tonight and how it was going to work out, even though they only had days left Summer was hoping for a miracle as in getting the tracking button on Mr Slimm's jacket. After long cool gin and tonics, or as Simon would say 'high balls', and he would often say after four of these your pie bold. Summer insisted they could only have a couple as they're heads needed to be clear. The evening had somewhat crept up on them and the stage was now set. The passports with the car hire details were conveniently placed on the table next to the empty gin and tonic glasses. Summer placed one of her eyeliner pencils behind the door just as she pulled the door shunt, this was something they could check on later when they got back to the room to collect the right button to match Mr Slimm's jacket. After making their way to the lobby bar, they noticed Mr Slimm's female bodyguard waiting in the corner. On noticing them, she walked over towards where they were now sitting.

"You are Mr and Mrs Bay, is that correct?"

"Yes, we are Simon," said as he pulled the stool up to get him closer to the bar.

"You have booked a table in the veto bar."

"Yes, we have; is there a problem?"

She then stopped what she was saying and apologised for the way she had presented herself and continued to say, "Mr Slimm would like to join you after dinner."

"Sorry," Summer said, "who?"

"Mr Slimm would like to join you after dinner." She then waited for a reply after saying it for the second time.

Simon then said, "But we only have a table booked for two."

"That's all been taken care of."

"In what way?" Summer said. "You now have a table booked for three, he will come to your table when he's ready." She then left the bar not saying another word, they both watched as she walked out.

"There goes our element of surprise."

Simon put his glass down on the bar. "How does he know our names?"

Summer made sure she had left before turning to him. "Bailey, of course, it can only be him, but nevertheless you're right there goes our ace card; we can only try and make it to our advantage."

"But what about her? She's a strange one."

"I don't think she's one to be messed with."

And they were right, she was a quiet person and didn't really know how to hold a conversation it just wasn't her way, when something needed to be said it was said by her in an abrupt manner. Her frame was athletic. Her hair cut just above the shoulders as not to get in her way. Her eyes were dark brown and stared right through you as if she was reading your every thought. She would only wear suits with a blouse no tie, as again it would get in the way Summer didn't like her there was something that just wasn't right, she couldn't read her.

Simon agreed and then said, "Have you realised she hasn't given her name."

The veto bar and restaurant were down the very end of the hotel lobby; it was situated three metres away from the main doors. Two bell boys looked after the doors of the restaurant as well as the hotel entrance doors, they both welcomed Simon and Summer as they approached the cooling air of the air conditioning as they stepped inside, a very energetic and polite floor manager asked for their names.

"Mr Bay, ah yes sir, please step this way."

Summer looked around the room taking everything in as she had done many times before, she then spotted Bailey sat at a table with the three other men, Mr Slimm was two tables down sitting with four men and of course, his female minder. Simon was shown to their own table which was fairly close to Mr Slimm, because they were that close to him they couldn't really talk in case something in their conversation was picked up on. Summer devised a cunning plan. She would take Simon's hand, and hold it looking in to his eyes as if she was being intimate but really she would be talking about Mr Slimm.

“Have you noticed he’s wearing a light blue jacket, and Bailey is sat with three bodyguards on the next table.”

Simon then took her other hand. “Yes, I’ve noticed, and he has his female minder with him, how are we going to do this, how on earth are we going to get away with this now.”

Summer looked around the restaurant again only to see Bailey lifting his glass to her, she nodded at him and looked back to Simon. “You’re right, it’s going to be difficult. Very difficult.” As the evening went by, Summer kept a watch full eye on Mr Slimm’s table his guest left one by one throughout the evening and then a bottle of cognac came to their table, shortly followed by Mr Slimm and closely behind his minder.

“May I join you?” His eyes were all over Summer. He sat himself down before they could reply to his request putting his hand up to stop his female minder following him. “It’s finally nice to meet you, my dear.” His accent was hard to place although he spoke English, with a hint of German as well, he placed his hands out in front of him gesturing.

“Please have your cognac.”

“Please join me.” Simon wasted no time he needed a stiff drink something to pluck up his courage raising the glass to his mouth as the cognac touched his lips.

He heard him say, “I know of you Mr Bay and of your reputation.”

Simon calmly put his glass down on the table the cognac still burning his lips the only thing he could do was to simply take it as a compliment. “Thank you, Mr Slimm,” Simon said as the glass touched his lips for the second time.

“So, why Rhodes?”

“And why not?” Simon said as he was now getting into character.

Summer looked at him. “Calm down, dear. You know you’re here on doctor’s orders so let’s not get upset.”

Simon looked at her and then back at Mr Slimm. “Go on, you were saying?”

Simon’s gamble had paid off, Mr Slimm smiled and said again, “Your reputation precedes you.” Simon raised his glass and smiled back at him as more cognac was poured as Mr Slimm in an unsuspecting way started to interrogate him as Summer could only look on. Hours had past as the restaurant slowly emptied to the point where there were the only three tables left in the restaurant with the floor manager eagerly waiting for them to leave. The staff just waited around the tables occasionally looking down at their watches without Mr Slimm noticing, and then Summer made her move.

She laughed out loud as she said, “I do think you’ve had a little bit too much Cognac, darling.” And then saying, “Please excuse me, I need to go back to my room, shan’t be long.”

Simon stood up as he took her hand. “OK, my dear.” He then carried on talking to Mr Slimm, pouring yet more cognac under the watchful eye of Mr Slimm’s female minder. As Summer walked down the hallway to their room, she could smell a very faint odour. She knew what it was straight away it was the cheap aftershave that Bailey used. She placed her key card through the key slot and then slowly pushed open the door to their room, just enough to slip her hand around the bottom of the door; it wasn’t there it had moved. Her eyeliner pencil had been pushed back against the wall. Once she was inside, she checked the passports on the table. They had been moved but nevertheless they were still there everything was still in its place. Her next move was to pick the button and thread to the nearest colour that would match Mr Slimm's jacket. She placed the needle and thread through the inside of her dress sleeve and then through one of the small holes in the button and then back through her dress sleeve to hold it in place for later, now that was done she sprayed herself with perfume and in no time, she was back at the table in the veto bar restaurant. By this time, Mr Slimm's eyes were rolling back in to his head. Simon had done his bit. Bailey and the other three bodyguards waited as did his female minder as Mr Slimm was beginning to slur his words, his posture slumping heavily forward.

Summer placed her hand on him under the watchful eye of his minder. "It's time we got you back to your room. I'll take your jacket."

Simon got to his feet looking at Summer only to be told, "NO, sit back down both of you sit down." Mr Slimm then turned to Bailey. "They're both coming to my room for one last drink."

Simon looked at Summer moving his eyes over to where his female minder and Bailey and the other bodyguards were sitting then nodded at Summer it was an agreeing nod, Bailey straight away took Mr Slimm's jacket from the chair, Summer's eyes fixed as the jacket was taken away from her, she was so close. The look on the floor manager's face said it all as the three bodyguards got Mr Slimm to his feet his female minder gave the staff large tips for their patience, and then they were all in formation his female minder set the following. She was at the front leading the way with the three bodyguards around Mr Slimm keeping him upright then it was Simon and Summer and at the rear was Bailey. They were now making their way to the penthouse suite, the walk back to Mr Slimm's room was slow which gave Summer time to think this through, the plan wouldn't work if Simon was in the room with her, because if he was, then Bailey or Mr Slimm's female minder would have to be there which would make it in possible to change the button on his jacket, she took Simon's hand and quietly said to him so Bailey couldn't hear.

"You have to go back to our room for this to work. Trust me, I'll be all right."

A short time later, just as they were about to enter the lift Simon stepped back bumping into Bailey. "You go on, darling. I have to go back to our room, I think I may have left the passports on the table, better to be safe than sorry." They all looked at him. Mr Slimm put his hand up to wave him away, it was a drunken pitiful wave. Bailey then let him pass as he knew he was telling the truth, because he had already seen them on their table. Simon now had a long walk, it was short in distance but long in his mind he did nothing else but think of Summer, he couldn't believe what he had just done. He had just walked out on his wife leaving her there with a stranger, and a dangerous stranger at that, he closed his room door as his eyes started to well up.

The lift door opened as Mr Slimm's female minder stepped out first she then moved her hand forward to one of the three bodyguards indicating for him to go ahead and check out Mr Slimm's room, she then waited at the lift with the rest until he opened the door, as he walked in to the room she once again indicated to them to start walking slowly towards the room, Summer then noticed she and the two bodyguards now had guns in their hands, slowing down as they approach the door, they were only seconds away when the bodyguard reappeared signalling everything's OK. Mr Slimm and

Summer entered the room with his minder and Bailey closed behind leaving the other two of his bodyguards outside at the door and the third was now back at the lift door covering. Mr Slimm insisted on more cognac as Bailey put the jacket over the back of the chair once the cognac was poured. Mr Slimm insisted Bailey and his minder leave the room. Bailey disagreed with this only to be told to get the hell out in an aggressive manner. They both left and Summer could see the look on their faces. This wasn't good; there was no way they could protect him. They were not happy with his decision. Summer then watched as they closed the door, now she was alone with him and didn't know what to expect from this sleaze ball; she was polite to towards him but still keeping her distance as she steadily manoeuvred herself around the room trying to keep one step ahead of him. She now suggested they have a drink on the balcony. This was a defensive move on her part as she could always lock him outside if needed. Mr Slimm fell back into his chair; his body was heavy with the cognac. Summer's plan was to get as much as she could down him it would make it easier for her to do the job she had to do and then get out of that room in one piece.

A good 30 minutes had past and another four cognacs in Mr Slimm had done its job. Summer put her glass down on the table and looked at him. What a pathetic man he was. He reigned with fear but if they all could see him now they would see how pathetic he really was. She called his name and then shook his arm but to no avail she then sat back in to the chair and finished her drink, time was ticking on she had to make her move. Thinking fast, she got up pushing the chair back along the tiled floor.

Mr Slimm woke from his sleep calling out, "Marianne!"

There was a knock on the door. “Sir, is everything OK?”

Summer had no choice but to open it, but she now had a name to the person, Marianne was his female minder, she stood at the door waiting. “Sir, is everything OK? Sir, can you hear me is everything OK?”

Summer stepped back. “He’s fine, we were just talking about you.”

She looked at Summer, Bailey interrupted, “Marianne, let it be. You can see he’s OK. We don’t need to get his back up do we?”

She then said thank you as she closed the door in her face. Summer rested her back against the door trying to listen in on the conversation on the other side.

Mr Slimm then moved getting to his feet it was all going wrong, she moved quickly across the room back to the balcony. “Please let me help you, are you OK?” muttered words came from his mouth, as she took his arm to support him, you need to lie down, his body was heavy as his feet were dragging back across the room as Summer was making loud laughter to confuse Bailey and Marianne who were still stood outside. It took some time to get him to the bedroom and once there, Summer managed to get him on the bed rolling him on his side so he didn’t choke in his sleep. At last now was the time to sew the button on to his jacket. She thought the best place to do this would be in the bathroom out of his sight once there. She could hear him moaning. It took Summer a good five minutes to change the button on his jacket, sewing the new button in to place and then the old one back on to her sleeve, and all the time listening to Mr Slimm”s moans. She was more concerned about him giving the game away then anything, but then he just stopped.

"Thank goodness for that," she said to herself as she tidied up the bits of thread making sure everything was in its place before going back into the bedroom. To her horror, she noticed Mr Slimm had been foaming from his mouth and was now lying motionless on the bed, she checked his pulse, then his airway. There was nothing, nothing could be done for him. He was dead. He must have had a seizure. Unknown to Summer, Mr Slimm suffered with epilepsy and this one was so severe he had swallowed his tongue resulting in him choking to death. She stepped back and looked at him and then thought what a fitting end for someone who rains down terror on others. She gathered her thoughts and then realised the predicament she was now in as she held his jacket in her low voice she said, "Well, he won't be needed this now." But now Summer needed to find a way out of there, first thing was to go to the room door. Once there, she put her ear to it and held her breath all she could hear was her own heart beating. She turned around to the bedroom the door still open slightly. Come on, Summer, think. Her plan was to get to the lift and then take it from there, she had to think quickly. The first port of call was to make it look as if he was asleep and that meant undressing him and setting the scene so she put some soft music on in the room system and then went back into the bedroom; there he was as before. In her head, she was hoping that he may have moved but it wasn't to be; he was definitely dead.

This was so surreal for Summer now, now she was undressing a dead man, a man who was the head of a drug cartel. First of all, she stripped him down to his underwear. She noticed the battle scars on his body that had healed over time. Looking around the room, Summer noticed his clothes were thrown over the back of chairs and his night wear was just dropped on the floor near his bed. OK what next she said to herself, bathroom. She ran a face cloth under the tap and then wiped his face down getting rid of any body fluids then cleaned the rest of him but then she struggled to get his nightwear on but perseverance paid off in the end. Summer had now placed him into his bed. Then she once again sat down with the soft music still playing. She now had to think for a moment, how was she going to get away with it. Summer then looked at the front door and then back at the bedroom door with the hallway doors opened. Her head was spinning. If she kept the bedroom door open, then when she opened the front door anybody outside of the room would be able to see straight through to the bedroom. It was a long shot but that's all she had so with that in mind, she made her way to the front door looking back to the bedroom. Yes, this could work. Now that her mind was made up. She made her way back to the bedroom for one last look around just to make sure everything was in place. It was as good as Summer could get it. Now she had to make it as realistic as she could for when she opened the front door to the bodyguards. It was now or never for her. There was no going back. She needed to get out of there and get out fast. Summer ran her fingers through her hair and then looked in to the hallway mirror, no not enough she did it once again then she pulled the zip halfway down on the back of her dress then kicked off her shoes and held them in her right hand. Again she looked back in to the bedroom one last time. Mr Slimm was sat upright but laying back slightly just as she had left him. Now she took a deep breath and then opened the door. Bailey and Marianne had gone just leaving the two bodyguards at the door and the other watching the lift. She pulled back the door as far as it would go the bodyguards turned to her. "Excuse me," she said as she pushed her way through. "That was embarrassing, he fell asleep on me and he's supposed to be a Casanova." Summer laughed then dropped her shoes on the floor and awkwardly manoeuvred her feet into them trying to keep their attention on her and not Mr Slimm, she then asked one of them to zip her dress up as she began to close the door but one of the bodyguards got to the door handle first. "Thank you, you're so kind," she said as she walked to the lift trying to breathe slowly for one minute it seemed it was all going her way but then the man at the lift stepped forward to stop her as Summer turned to the two at the door. "He's sleeping like a baby. I'm sure he would rather forget about tonight, so are you sure you really want to go in and wake him up?" She stopped and waited. "Well, come on, I haven't got all night what's it to be?" She waited looking at the two of them at the door then turning back to the one at the lift. They slowly pulled the door shut Summer had got away with it. Well, got away with it for now. It wasn't over not by a long way. The bodyguards then signalled it was OK for her to use the lift. Summer was now safe in the lift both palms of her hands were pushing against the doors. As she leaned forward, she stood there in a quiet state but yet she was screaming inside as the automated voice of the lift doors opening brought her back around, lobby. Summer quickly gathered her thoughts as she walked out of the penthouse suite lift and made her way to one of the two lifts on the other side of the lobby trying not to draw attention to herself as hard as it was. Again she was in the relative safety of a lift. Once more she only had a matter of metres to go when the lift doors opened, she wanted to scream again but as before she was still screaming inside as she turned the last corner, now she could see the safety of her room door, she could see sanctuary well for now anyway.

Simon jumped up from his chair as the door opened Summer just stood there kicking the door shut behind her with her heel. Simon put his arms around her.

"My God, are you OK? You look terrible." Summer stood there motionless her eyes rolling upwards she just didn't have the answer to what he had just said, even now he was still putting his almighty foot in it, again Simon said, "Are you OK? Did you get away with it?"

"Well…yes and no," Summer said as she pulled away.

"Just let me breathe."

Simon looked at her as he sat back down. "Tell me."

"Well, I managed to get the button on his jacket."

Simon interrupted. "Well, that's great. The job's done then."

There was a silence in the room.

"Tell me, Summer. Just tell me."

She looked at him. "Mr Slimm is dead."

Chapter 6

Simon was standing there, shell-shocked, rubbing his knees, trying to take in what she said.

"I've told you. He's dead. One minute he was there the next minute he wasn't."

Simon started to walk around the room. "What are we going to do?" He poured a large glass of whiskey but then didn't taste a drop, he looked at Summer again. "Do you think if we come clean it would help?"

Summer looked at him; this was the jump start she needed. She felt as if she had been coasting in neutral but was now back in first gear. "Get your flight case and put a change of clothes in it and then put something casual on to go in, then empty the safe." Summer did the same. She then opened the secret zip in her makeup case taking the passports out and placed them in her shoulder bag as she tuned to Simon.

"Where's the passports for Mr and Mrs Bay?"

Simon zipped his case up. "They're still in the safe. We don't need them now, do we?"

Summer explained to him, "As we stand now, there are maybe five people that know us by sight. If we leave the passports, there will be a hell of a lot more, so get the passports and all the jewellery as well."

On that note, Simon quickly took the passports from the safe. “That makes sense,” he said.

Summer took one last look around the room before leaving. “We came in with so much and now were leaving with so little,” she said as she picked up the sliver foil from a champagne bottle on their way out of the room.

“What’s that for?” Simon asked.

“I’ve seen this trick online. It’s amazing what you come across when you have some time on your hands.” She placed the foil on to one edge of her key card and then placed the card carefully into the card lock on the door and then very slowly pulling the card out a bit at a time making sure the foil stayed in place. It worked. The foil was now wedged into the door lock she then put a do not disturb sign on the door handle. The hotel was a peaceful place in the early hours of the morning and anybody in their right minds would be tucked up in bed and that’s what they were both banking on. They slowly made their way to the lift and within minutes, they were in the main lobby, both looking to the left as they came out of the lift. There was nobody on the reception desk. They now moved swiftly across the floor and through the main doors a single bell boy opened it for them. It was so peaceful outside. Summer looked up to where Mr Slimm’s penthouse suite was. The light was still on.

Simon took her hand. “It’s done now. Come on, we need to get going we need to get as far away from this place as we can.”

There were two taxis waiting on the corner and a small bus parked at the bus stop. Simon said, “I don’t think a taxi is a good idea, do you?”

Summer was already on it. She was already on her way to talk to the bus driver. "What time will you be setting off?"

In his broken English, the driver replied, "Now, if you wish." Without further ado, they both got on. Sitting at the back, they sat there as the bus driver started his engine the interior lights dimmed and then came back to life as he revved the engine up.

"So, what do we do now?"

Summer put their flight bags on the seat in front of them. "We need to get off this island, that's the first thing and we can't trust anyone you do know all hell is going to break loose when they go into Mr Slimm's room later on this morning." Simon undid his jacket as he got comfortable in his seat.

"They're all going to be looking for us we need to ring the Fat Club." He twisted the ring around his finger as he looked at Summer.

"We have to lie low for a couple of days to test the water."

Simon interrupted her. "But we need to ring in so they can get us out of here."

Their conversation was briefly interrupted by the driver. "Are you on a day trip?"

"Yes," Summer said as she got up from her seat and sat next to the bus driver leaving Simon sat at the back. "Your island is so lovely, it's a beautiful place."

This opened the driver up to her and in his broken English he started to talk about the island. "Have you seen Xapaki?" Summer asked him to say it again.

"Xapaki." He then pointed to the paper map that was placed on the front of his dashboard. "It's good, nice place, very beautiful, very quiet, not lot of people."

Summer asked how far away it is, she then pointed to the map. "Here to here. How far?"

"One hour, maybe a little more," he said.

Summer then asked, "Do you know of a hotel?"

"Yes, of course. But you only go for to see the beach."

"Beautiful beach, yes." Summer asked again, "But is there a hotel?"

And again, the bus driver said, "Yes, of course."

Summer made her way back to Simon moving for side to side as the bus travelled alone the uneven road constantly dodging the potholes, she sat back down next to him. "We're going to a place called Xapaki. It's on the other side of the island and it's quiet, which is a good thing, and there's a hotel there, so that will give us a bit of time to sort things out."

As the bus came closer to Xapaki, the driver called out, "Mrs, Mrs, come to me." Summer once again held the handrails on the top of the seats as she made her way to the driver. "Have you eaten?" the driver said as Summer found the safety of the seat next to him.

"No, we haven't."

He then nodded. "I have breakfast, you two have breakfast with me, yes?" Summer agreed straight away as the driver pulled both his hands up from the steering wheel to indicate 10 minutes while's steering with his knees. The bus came to a stop outside a small house hiding away in the shelter of some olive trees, rays of sunlight found their way through the branches and even at that time in the morning the sun was hot it was so beautiful it was hard to believe what they had both just gone through the night before and now they were in a beautiful place like this. The driver sat them both down at a small table outside with freshly cut flowers placed in the middle, he then called out mama. A fresh-faced, somewhat rounded lady came out to greet him placing her hands on his cheeks. She then said something in Greek to him and Summer could tell it was something affectionate from mother to son she called him by his name which was Spiros, his mother then looked across to where Simon and Summer were sitting and smiled at them. They're table was filled with cheese, olives, bread and fruit and cold fruit juice. A good 40 minutes had past when Spiros came back outside with his little boy who was also called Spiros he was going to be their interpreter for what was about to come next. Father and son sat down at the table. The father then said something in Greek to his son and then the very polite and well-mannered boy told Simon and Summer.

"My father is a bus driver this is his business, my name is Spiros as is my father," he continued to say, "English is one of my subjects at school, my father asks are you both in trouble?" Simon looked at Summer. "My father says you both looked worried when you got on his bus." Simon put his piece of bread back on his plate as the boy continue to translate. "You have to be honest with yourself and my father, this is a bad hotel where you were staying." What he was saying was this was one of Mr Slimm's side lines. He continued to say, "Bad men run this hotel, is that why you were leaving?" Simon knew by the look on Summer's face she was going to say something. He placed his hand on her knee to stop her.

"It's OK, Simon," she said. "I can tell these are good people."

Summer came clean. "Yes, you're right."

The boy translated back to his father, his father then raised his hands and said, "Kalós."

Summer told him they had been on holiday the year before and was invited back only to find it wasn't what it seemed, it turned out they wanted us to take something back to England for them, and now we don't know what to do. Summer had told him what he wanted to hear which was the truth in her eyes and that was all he needed to know.

"So they're going to be looking for you now, and this is why you got on my father's bus," the boy said.

Summer nodded then looked at Simon.

"Because you have both been honest with my father, he has said he will look after you for two nights. My uncle has the hotel nearby and he has agreed to let you stay for two nights. On the third day, he has a boat going over to Athens, he will take you, then you will have to go your own way."

Simon looked down at his watch as the young boy's eyes opened wide.

There was still know sign of Mr Slimm. Bailey had just arrived at the door to his room only to find the bodyguards still there.

"What's happening?" They were concerned just as much as he was. Bailey then knocked on the door but there was no response.

"You get down to reception and get a pass card for the room."

As the lift door opened, the bodyguard was pushed aside by Marianne, she walked towards the door shouting 'is he up yet', she could tell by the look on Bailey's face something wasn't right as she held her card key up in her hand asking Bailey and the second bodyguard stepped back away from the door, the light turned green from red as the door was pushed open. Bailey Stopped the bodyguard from entering as he closed it behind them, he then looked down the hallway to the bedroom to where Mr Slimm was sitting upright in bed, he knew it wasn't good. He looked at Marianne the look on her face was enough. They both knew he was dead. He was of a grey in colour and lips slightly blue. There was no hope for him. Marianne looked around the front room first, everything was there that she knew of but Bailey knew that smell of perfume they closed the bedroom door and then asked the bodyguard outside to come in. He stood there alone in the hallway, agitated and alarmed as to what was going on, Bailey calmed him down and reassure him nothing is going to happen to him.

"Tell me what time did Mrs Bay leave the room?"

"It was about one, maybe two hours or so after you both left."

"Did you hear Mr Slimm at any time?"

"Well, yes and no."

Marianne jumped in. "What do you mean? You either did or you didn't. What is it?"

"She was on edge." The bodyguard stepped back against the hallway wall, once again Bailey calmed him telling Marianne to back off.

"So, when you said yes and no what did you mean?"

"It was the music, and I could hear Mrs Bay laughing and speaking to him and then the door opened. I could see Mr Slimm sitting up in bed I called his name, but he didn't answer me I took it to be because of the music that he didn't hear me." Marianne said, "Why didn't you enter the room?"

"I tried to, but Mrs Bay said I wouldn't do that as he wasn't in the best of moods and wanted to be left alone and then she pulled the door shut."

"Then what did you do."

"We both stayed at the door."

Bailey put his hand on the bodyguard's shoulder reassuring him. "You did good, now wait outside and don't let anybody in."

The door closed behind him as Bailey and Marianne opened the bedroom door once more. Bailey pulled the sheets back on the bed Marianne said, "He's been washed down."

Bailey agreed. "We have to check everything just to make sure nothing has been taken." He then said, "We keep the body in the room. This cannot get out, not yet, and you need to get your story straight."

Marianne pulled the sheets back over him. "You're loving this, aren't you?"

Bailey turned to her. "You're his personal bodyguard. You should have been here, this shouldn't have happened, you came into the organisation two years ago, you were his little blue-eyed girl."

"Well, not anymore." Marianne made her way out of the room and into the lift and then over to Simon and Summer's room closely followed by Bailey. Once there, they noticed the do not disturb sign on the door, Marianne knocked frantically but to no avail, as they were both deciding what to do next one of the hotel maids asked if they needed any help. Bailey asked if she had a pass card as they had mislaid theirs. She was only happy to help, she placed the card into the reader. It beeped twice with two red flashes, she tried again it was the same as before. Marianne pushed her to one side and in her anger and frustration she kicked the door open with one kick. The maid stood there in astonishment as Bailey and Marianne entered the room, it was empty the safe opened with its contents missing, Marianne checked the wardrobe everything was still there but some of their belongings were thrown across the bed.

Bailey said, "It looks like they've made a quick exit and you need to catch up with them your life may depend on it."

Summer asked young Spiros to ask his father why he was really helping them.

"Giatí na tous voithoún," his father replied to his comments.

"My father says they have been our family's enemies for many years." He then said something to his son. "We have to go now; my father will drop you both at the hotel on my way to school." Again, the boy looked at Simon's watch as it glistened in the sunlight.

"OK we go now," Spiros said as he said his goodbye to his mama as she stood in the doorway waving everybody off, Simon and Summer sat at the back of the bus with young Spiros they talked about his school and his ambitions in life. "We are here." Summer looked out of the side window. The hotel was situated on a small hill in the town it wasn't that big but it still over towered the other buildings nearby, fully grown trees enhance its appearance. Spiros parked his small bus on the hotel driveway next to the turning circle and then asked his son to wait on the bus.

"Come, come." Simon and Summer followed him into the reception area, again he spoke in Greek smiling as he did so to the lady on the desk, then turning to Simon and then kissing Summer on her cheek. "You will be good now, yes." Summer took this to mean they would be safe now but for how long as they were still on the island.

The person on reception smiled at them again saying, "Your room is on the fourth floor, room number is 62." She passed Simon the key as Summer looked around. The hotel was a delightful little place they could tell it was a family run hotel, the reception area was part of the restaurant, as they would put the tables out at set times for the guests. The bar itself was placed in the corner but also ran outside as a pool bar this was nothing like the hotel they have just left, no pompous people trying to outdo each other and as much as Summer wanted that life style now she had experienced it she was now realising it wasn't all that she thought it would be.

The day had moved on and now they were in the midday sun, as Simon couldn't resist saying mad Dogs and Englishmen. Summer just raised her eyebrows in disbelief, the hotel was coming alive with the enthusiastic holiday makers busily going about their business, and because of this they both found it hard to make any eye contact in fear of being caught. Their room was of a modest size, a room with two single beds with drag marks on the carpet where over time the bed had been pulled together to make a double bed by previous holidaymakers. A dressing table with a statue of the Virgin Mary and a small petite vase filled with flowers from the hotel garden next to it. The dressing table itself was placed on one side of the room pushed against the wall Summer looked across to where the balcony was a table with two chairs placed nearby, as she looked behind her she seen a small bathroom next to the main door. Simon looked out from the balcony on to the bay, it was hard to believe that from the road, the hotel looked like any other, but looking out from the rear on to the beautiful bay, it was just so beautiful. The hotel itself was situated on the clifftop that dropped in to the sea the

1980's infinity pool was placed so close to the edge that it actually looked like you would topple over in the sea. He was just about to call Summer over when there was a knock on the door. Summer, listen closely for anybody talking outside as Simon came closer to her not saying word, somebody tapped again.

"Room service! This is your room service."

They waited, Simon looking back at the balcony as Summer took a tight hold of his hand. "Don't be silly, you'll never make the fall."

She then reluctantly and with great care to avoid any dangerous moves and with Simon already with his shoulder pushed against the door ready to take any sudden impact as Summer opened it a little, she then let out a sigh of relief.

"Hello, my name is Bernus. May I come in? You know of

Spiros, he is my uncle."

Their faces changed from frowns to smiles.

"My uncle has told me you are in some sort of trouble."

Simon answered straight away. "Yes, we are. Can you help?"

Summer then took Simon's hand yet again as she said, "You see, it's the not knowing."

Bernus stopped them. "You're safe here. No one knows you're here," he continued to say, "we're going to keep you here for two nights and on the third day, you will go to Athens by boat that's as far as we can take you."

Simon and Summer smiled with reassurance, he continued to say, "It's crucial you stay around the hotel till you go, the less people see of you, the better chance you will have of getting away with this, do you understand?"

Summer agreed with him and then asked, “Your English is very good.”

“Thank you, I’m studying law at university in England, I always come home for holidays. You both will be meeting Alessandro, my father, on your stay here, just be aware his

English isn’t that good.”

Simon asked, “How do we pay you?”

“You don’t, like I said Spiros told me you’re both in trouble and our family have a long-term feud with that family you’re running from so therefore you are here as our guests.”

Bernus then wished them a good day and then made his way back to reception, they hugged each other as Simon said, “Sorry.”

Summer put her arms around him squeezing him tight saying, “Sorry for what? I’m the one that wanted to do this.”

“Yes, but if I hadn’t had gone online with the fat club in the first place, then we wouldn’t be here in this mess now.”

They stayed in the safety of their room for the rest of the day people watching from their balcony, and as Simon looked out on to the bay, he realised just how far away from home they really were. The evening was soon upon them they had eaten and we’re now having a glass of wine in their room when Summer got up and walked over to the balcony.

“What’s wrong?”

She turned looking back at him. “It looks like the hotel is having a pool bar party.”

Simon followed her over to the balcony putting his arm around her then kissing her softly on her cheek, in turn, Summer turned to him putting her cheek against his, he then suggested he go down to the hotel bar and pick up a couple more bottles of wine Summer nodded her head.

The hotel restaurant was so alive that evening the pool bar party was now in full swing when Simon bumped into Bernus. "Hello, Simon. Is everything OK?"

Simon smiled. "Yes, we're doing what you asked of us. We're staying in the room."

Bernus looked outside at the pool party and then looked at Simon. "Why don't you and your wife come down to the party."

Simon looked back at him. "But you said we have to keep a low profile."

"Yes, you're right, I did say that but this is a hotel only party and as long as you both stay in the hotel grounds tonight, you will be OK. We'll talk in the morning."

Simon smiled as he picked up his wine from the bar and made his back to their hotel room where Summer was still standing on the balcony a light breeze blew her long hair back in to the room as she swayed slowly to rhythm of the music, Simon could only look she was as gorgeous now as she was when they first met.

"I have the wine," he said as he placed it on the table. "We can drink it later."

"Later? Why later?" Summer was somewhat puzzled as Simon took her hand.

"Come on, we're going to the pool party."

She pulled back. "What are you doing! Are you mad?"

Simon once again removed her doubts. "It's OK. I bumped into Bernus in the bar, he said the pool party is only for the hotel residents, so therefore, it would be safe for us to join in as long as we don't leave the hotel."

"So what are we waiting for?" Summer loosened her grip. Are you sure? His eyes said it all and she knew now it would be safe.

The wind had picked up a little as they both danced under the moonlight and as they did so the sea breeze climbed the cliff face creating light ripples across the infinity pool, it was so welcoming and for a short time, it blew their worries away as they danced into the night.

Summer said in a soft hushed tone, "This is how it should be. Just you and nobody else matters." Simon held her tight their bodies pushed firmly together as they moved from side to side for the last dance of the evening. Simon was the first to wake the following morning his eyes open and was fixated on the glass of water that he had placed next to his bed the night before, he watched as the beads of water ran down the inside of the glass making their way to the bottom, making its way home, and that's where he wanted be, home, home with Summer.

"Penny for them."

Simon turned over to Summer, she said again. "Penny for them." And then smiled at him.

"I do think we need to ring this number to let them know what's gone on, and that we need their help."

Summer agreed this time. "Yes, you're right, let's ring down for breakfast and then we'll let them know that we're getting off the island by boat."

Breakfast of the day was somewhat of a light one and was soon devoured. They had both decided to ring the number from the hotel lobby as Summer thought it was best to leave their mobile phones behind at the last hotel. The reception was quiet most of the hotel residents were out for day, only a select few of die-hard sunbathers commanded the pool area. Simon asked if he could use the phone and was then pointed in the direction of a small kiosk where a phone was placed inside for some privacy. He took the ring off his finger and then dialled the number from inside it, they waited, the person on the other end of the line was straight to the point.

"What is the small symbol opposite the third number on the outside of the ring?"

Summer picked up the ring. "Tell them it's a rose bud."

"What is the last four digits of your code?"

Simon counted on his fingers till he got to the last four digits, again there was silence.

"Putting you through now." "They're putting me through now." Summer nodded at him.

"Jessica here, where are you?" Summer put her ear close to Simon's so she could hear what was being said. "Can you hear me? Where are you now?"

Simon replied, "We need help. We need to get out."

"I know you do, tell me where you are."

"We're in a small place call Xapaki."

"Where in Xapaki are you staying?"

Summer put her finger on the receiver cutting Simon off.

"Summer! What are you doing? Why did you do that?" She replied to him, "Didn't you hear what she said?"

"Yes, of course I did. She asked where we were staying! What's up with that?"

"No," Summer said. "She said she knows we need help. How could she know we need help because as far as I'm aware nobody knows he's dead yet."

Simon then placed his own finger on the receiver tapping it frantically. "My God, what are we going to do now?"

Marianne was running around the hotel looking for any clues as to where they were when her phone rang.

"Hello. Yes of course I'm still looking. No, not really. Of course, I'm sure. Are you kidding? Where? How do you know this? OK, I'll make my way over there, but I hope your information is right because I don't want you wasting my time."

It was short and sweet. Marianne then rang Bailey. "Where are you."

"I'm on the boat with Mr Slimm."

"What?"

"I'll rephrase, we're on the boat with Mr Slimm. He's in a bag, we're trying to decide what to do. We're just waiting for the call from the boss so we can go ahead."

It was ironic that only days ago, Mr Slimm had ordered the hit on one of the men at the hotel who eventually became fish bait, and now here was Mr Slimm awaiting the same fate. "So how long are you going to be?"

"As long as it takes. Do you think I enjoy sitting in a boat in the middle of the ocean? I hate the ocean, in fact, I hate anything where you have to get wet. Tell me what's up?"

"I've had a call. Mr and Mrs Bay are on the other side of the island, in a place called Xapaki."

"OK, make your way over and stay in touch with me. I'll get to you as soon as I've fed the fish."

Simon and Summer were now sitting on the balcony. "So what do we do?" Simon said as he rubbed his knees.

"Look, it's nearly midday," Summer said, trying to reassure him. "We only have six, maybe seven hours before we meet Alessandro and then we'll know what time we go in the morning. Come on, Simon, we've come this far let's see this through." He looked at the bottle on the side, Summer stopped him. "No, that's not the answer and definitely not a good idea. We need to keep a clear head tonight."

Marianne was now on her way to Xapaki when her phone rang.

"Yes, I'm on my way. I'll be there as soon as I can. I know I can't let them get off the island, either way I'll get them don't worry, it's not just your head it's mine as well."

Simon found it hard to believe that the world was still going on around them. People were going about their holiday laughing and joking around the pool a far cry from what they were both going through. How he longed to turn back the time and be sat at Teddy's desk and say no to his idea, even now he was still kicking himself for saying yes but he had now got them both in this mess, and the upshot was they were fighting to stay alive. He was just about to take Summer's hand when there was a light tap on their door. Simon looked towards the door as Summer put her finger on her lips to indicate to him to keep quiet, it tapped again they both looked.

"This is Bernus, are you there?"

Simon said to Summer, "My heart can't take much more of this."

Once inside, Bernus told them his father would be on the hotel grounds at six p.m. "He will be sitting at his table near the pool bar."

Summer asked what he looked like as they didn't want to bring any unwanted attention to themselves. Bernus politely replied, "White pants, striped shirt rolled up to his elbows and a white Panama hat, you only have one hour with him then you will know what time you go tomorrow." Summer wanted to tell him about what had happened today but thought better of it just in case they called the whole thing off.

Bernus was right about what his father was wearing they both found him straight away, they introduced themselves to him as he did to them. Alessandro took a sip of his espresso coffee followed by a sip of meataxe. "My son tells me you are both in trouble, yes?" He then put his hand up before Summer could answer his question, getting the attention of his son Bernus who was soon sat beside him. "You know my son, yes?"

They both nodded.

"My English is not that good, so I will talk through my son, yes?"

They both nodded.

Bernus said to Summer, "It's OK, just be honest."

Alessandro put his hand on Bernus cheek and pinched it saying, "O gios mou." He then smiled, his father then spoke in Greek for Bernus to translate. Summer told Bernus everything but not that they were working under cover for the fat club. The way it was put was that they were in the wrong place at the wrong time. Just over one hour past when

Alessandro asked Bernus, "Boreíte na tous pistévoun?" Then Bernus replied, "Nai, aftá eínai kaloí ánthropo." His father then smiled and nodded his head.

Bernus then turned to Simon and Summer saying, "You both go tomorrow at five a.m. in the morning."

Chapter 7

Things were looking up they were now in a better place. Bernus told them not to have any drink tonight as the boat journey was going to be long and hard. Summer took Simon's hand and squeezed it tightly. They were now finely going to get off the island.

Marianne had just arrived at Xapaki and had parked her car down one of the many small, cobbled streets. She was sitting outside a bar having yet another coffee to increase her energy levels, her eyes red with the lack of sleep as she had not slept since the death of Mr Slimm, little did she know she was barely but only ten minutes away from the hotel where Simon and Summer were staying. Xapaki was only a small place but nevertheless a somewhat lively one and Marianne had to find them and find them quickly so there was no time for sleeping. Her phone rang causing her to jump her nerves on edge unable to relax.

"We've had the go ahead to tip him over the side, where are you now?"

"I'm sitting outside a bar in Xapaki, asking the locals if they have seen anybody who fits their description."

"OK, is there a Harbour in Xapaki?"

"Yes, I'm looking at it from the bar."

Bailey explained the situation. “Mr Slimms going over the side as we speak, we then need to clean up here and then I’ll get the boys to drop me off at Xapaki Harbour.”

“I need to get off this damn boat, so I’ll see you in the morning that’s the best I can do.” Marianne had no choice but to say OK. Within minutes, she had another call.

“No, not yet. I know and my head is on the block as well as yours. I know they must not get back to England don’t you think I know that.”

Simon and Summer were now back in their room, their flight cases on the bed, not that they had anything to pack but what little they had was packed and ready to go when yet again there was a knock on the door.

“It is me. Bernus.” Simon opened the door and let him in, Summer could see something wasn’t right.

“What’s wrong, Bernus?”

“There’s a lady at a bar, not 10 minutes away asking questions. It looks like she’s looking for you.”

Simon said straight away, “It’s Marianne, it has to be.”

Bernus cut in on the conversation. “They must be searching the island for you both, you must stay in your room she is so close, be ready for 4 o’clock in the morning. I’ll knock twice on your door.”

Summer sat down on the chair whilst Simon walked around the room rubbing the back of his head in a distraught way saying, “This is unbearable, what else can possibly go wrong the cards are most definitely against us, this is killing me.” Summer stopped his moaning.

“Wait a minute, don’t you see?”

“See what?” Simon said as he sat on the bed.

"Don't you think it's a bit of a coincidence that she's turned up here, if she was searching for the ports and harbours she would be nowhere near us yet, but yet she's here now, why's that?"

Simon didn't need any prompting. "It's the phone call I made, isn't it?"

Summer nodded her head, and with that in mind she locked the door saying, "We really need to be careful now more than ever."

Time ticked away and the silence was unbearable, every hour they stayed in the room felt like two. Finally, it was late evening and Simon could not take anymore, his nerves were shot as he stood to his feet.

"We need to get to the phone down in reception."

Summer quickly sat him back down. "Why?"

"We need to speak with the only person I can trust."

Summer looked at him. "Do you mean, Teddy?"

He stood up again. "Yes."

"Then we both go down."

Simon stood his ground. "No, Summer, it's better if you stay here and let me do this. Let's be honest, it's only me that can get through to Teddy anyway."

Summer sat back down as she told him, "Be careful and don't take any chances."

"I promise, I won't." Getting down to the lobby was the easy part but once there, Simon's heart felt like it was beating out of his chest he looked towards the reception desk as she put her hand up to wave at him Simon waved back. That's all clear, he said to himself. Now all he had to worry about was the main door but then he thought the driveway was fairly long and the bottom of the road was some distance from the hotel. So if that was her only way in, then he would see her before she had seen him. He made his way to the phone once again waving at the receptionist as he picked up the receiver. The phone had a rotary dial and each number he dialled seemed like an eternity.

"Good evening, FAT."

Simon was straight to the point. "Put me through to Teddy, please."

"I'm sorry, sir, but I've been told not to disturb him tonight."

Simon answered back quite abruptly, "Just tell him it's Simon Rodgers, he'll want to speak to me, trust me." "Could I take your code number please." Without any hesitation, he gave it to her.

"Hold the line."

Teddy sat up in bed trying to get to his phone before it woke his wife up, but this was to no avail as she was now awake.

"This better be good," he said.

"Go back to sleep, dear. No, not you. What do you want?"
"Sir, I'm very sorry to ring you at home."

Teddy answered her, "But did I not say to you before I left for home, no calls."

"Yes, you did, sir, but this person was very persistent, and I told him to ring back in the morning, but he said you will want to speak to him."

Teddy turned on his side and was becoming agitated. "Well, tell me who this damn person is."

"It's Simon Rodgers, sir."

Teddy bolted upright. "Did you say Simon Rodgers?"

"Yes, sir."

Teddy's wife turned to him. "For God sakes, what are you doing?"

Teddy answered, "Go to sleep, dear. No not you, put Simon through to me now. Simon, is that you?" Teddy said as he jumped out of bed.

"Yes, sir, it's me."

"One minute," Teddy said as he closed the bedroom door and then stood on his landing. "What's happening, Simon?

Are you OK?"

Simon was relieved just to hear his voice.

"Did you manage to get the tracking button on Mr Slimms' jacket? Did everything go as planned?"

Simon turned around looking up and down the lobby before answering him.

"Where have you been? What do you mean, Simon?"

"Mr Slimm is dead and no it didn't go to plan."

There was an embarrassing silence on Teddy's behalf.

"You didn't know, did you Teddy?"

He came clean. "No, I didn't." Simon took the phone from his ear and looked down at it as he gritted his teeth in silence and then put the phone back to his ear.

"Where are you now?"

"We're on the run."

"Who have you been in touch with?"

Simon told him, "Well when we realised it had gone wrong and Mr Slimm was dead, we managed to get out of the hotel by the skin of our teeth and now we're on the other side of the island, we rang the number on the inside of my ring for some help to get off the island and back to England."

Teddy had gone into another bedroom and was now sitting on the edge of the bed go on, Simon continued,

"Eventually, we were put through to Jessica Green and I told her what had happened and where on the island we were. I was just about to tell her what hotel we were staying at when Summer put her finger on the receiver."

"Why did she do that?"

"Summer had picked up on the fact that she already knew Mr Slimm was dead."

Teddy put his head down. "Dear dear dear, this is not good not good at all, where are you now, Simon?"

"We're in a place called Xapaki."

"What hotel are you staying in?" Simon held his breath.

"You don't want to tell me, do you?" Teddy said, "I understand that, and I feel you've been let down."

Simon explained to him. "There's a woman called Marianne she is, or should I say was, Mr Slimm's personal bodyguard and she's here in Xapaki, not 10 minutes away from us."

"Right," Teddy said in his authoritative voice. "We need to get you off the island, we can't take the risk of flying you both out from Rhodes, they'll be watching the airport."

Simon cut in, "We're leaving the Island by boat tomorrow at four in the morning, but we have no idea what we're going to do when we get there."

"First of all," Teddy said, "where are they taking you?"

"To Athens."

"Can the people who are helping you be trusted?"

"Impeccably," Simon said. "Without their help, we would have been dead now."

"Good, so here's what I want you to do, get yourselves to Athens, do you have any money?"

"No, we don't."

"Do you have any of the jewellery on you?"

"Yes, we do."

"OK then. Sell what you have to and get yourself into a hotel that's out of the way then call me on my private number. Do you have a pen?"

Simon looked around the phone kiosk. He then told Teddy to wait as he asked the receptionist for a pen. Teddy gave him his number.

"I can only tell you both to take care and I promise I will get you back home trust me." He then put the phone down. Teddy had already put two and two together as he picked up his phone and dialled a number. "Is that you, Roland?" It was Sinclair.

"What's up, Teddy? It must be bad for you to ring me at this hour."

"It's Simon."

"What?"

"Simon Rodgers."

"He's not dead, is he?"

"No, but he soon will be, along with his wife Summer if we don't help him."

"Where is he?"

"Rhodes."

"Rhodes…what the hell."

Teddy stopped him. "I'll tell you all about it, but can you get to Athens? I'm already packing will it be a in and out job."

"Yes, but I must have this person called Marianne back in England I think she may be working for another department within the organisation but now under the supervision for Jessica Green, your tickets will be waiting at the airport desk

I'll text you the flight time on your way down and stay in touch."

"Teddy, are you coming back to bed?"

"Yes, dear, just one more call. Hello Charles, I hope I didn't get you out of bed."

"No, Teddy," Charles said standing in his en suite in his pyjama bottoms and slippers.

"Good, you're late up, Charles, you do know you're on an early call in the morning, you must get some sleep."

"Yes, Teddy, I will. What can I do for you?"

"Have you seen anything different about Jessica?"

"In what way?"

"Something's going on I just need to know has there been any changes in her attitude has she been unsettled in any way?"

Charles yawned as he said, "Yes, come to think of it she has been a bit on edge, but I just put that down to the way she's coping with the job."

"Teddy, are you coming to bed or not?"

"Yes, dear. Charles, I think for the next couple of days you should be prepared, do you know what I mean?"

"Yes sir, I will wear it at all times. Now, Teddy, do as your wife says and go back to bed good night."

Simon was now back in the safety of their hotel room where Summer had asked him what had gone on, he explained the reasons why it had taken so long.

"Teddy's told me to sell the jewellery and then book into a hotel that's out of the way, he wants me to ring him when we book in so he can arrange flights to get us both home."

Summer smiled with relief. All they needed to do now was get off the island. They didn't sleep that evening for reasons to be expected. The following morning soon came with two light taps on their door.

"It's Bernus, are you there?" Simon eagerly opened the door and in he stepped carrying a small holdall. "Are we OK to go?"

"Yes, we are," they both said.

Bernus pulled two pairs of overhauls from the bag and one cap. "Please put these on over your clothes." He then said to Summer, "You need to put your hair up and wear the cap."

Summer did as Bernus asked. "OK, now we are ready to go."

Bernus had already cleared a path from the hotel room to the car on the hotel car park, he had asked the lady on reception to sit in the back room until he came back, what she didn't see wouldn't put her in any unforeseen consequences.

Simon joked on their way through the reception area. "We need to stop doing a runner from hotels." Summer looked and smiled at him she could see the funny side to what he had just said but knew they weren't out of danger yet, once they were outside, Bernus looked up to the top of the hotel drive, he waited holding both his arms out to keep Simon and Summer at his side until the all clear was given by the person at the top of the road.

"This way," Bernus said pointing to the car on the carpark. "Please get in the back and stay down, you must remember people are out looking for you so you must stay down for the journey." Simon asked how long it is. "It's a 15-minute drive to the boat it's 15 minutes to keep you both alive."

Marianne was sat in a cheap hotel room a far cry from what she had been staying in. There wasn't any point in being out on the streets looking for them as everything was closed down. She waited patiently for Bailey's call and time was ticking away. She was now at her wits end and there was nothing she could do about it. Simon and Summer were now tucked away in the back of the car with Bernus driving; it was a clear run to the boat only the local fisher men were out at that time in the morning and Bernus knew the locals wouldn't say a word, and why wouldn't they, because Alessandro and his family owned the town. The boat that was taking them to the mainland was just one of the many boats that was doing illegal runs, nothing to over the top of course and certainly no drugs. Alessandro put a line under anything like that, and God help anybody if he caught them doing it, but as for people not saying anything will that was because they owned him their livelihoods as Alessandro set them up in their businesses and asked for nothing in return, just their loyalty, Bernus pulled slowly up to the boat where it was nesting in a small rocky bay out of the way of prying eyes with a young man waiting at the stern, the boat itself had two sturdy powerful engines that were built for speed. It was loaded to go and was just waiting for the rest of its cargo which was Simon and Summer. Bernus put his hand out to say goodbye but Summer was now so emotional all she could do was throw her arms around him kissing him on the cheek. He then turned to Simon. He asked Bernus how he could repay him, where Bernus just said, "I would like to think you would do the same for me and my family." Simon shook his hand but then took his watch off and handed it to Bernus who was now puzzled.

"Our journey started with a kind bus driver called Spiros, who took us both in out of kindness we then met his son who took a liking to my watch, please Bernus, give this watch to Spiros and though his son is too young to appreciate it now maybe his father will pass it down when he becomes of age." Bernus cupped Simon's hands with his own and said thankyou and then said, "Be safe in what you do and may the gods be with you both." As Simon and Summer climbed aboard the speedboat putting their life jackets on as they did so, there was that unmistakable sound of the V-8 engine rumbling as they both sat at the stern of the boat as it slowly pulled away from the rocky bay. Summer looked back one last time to see Bernus walking back to his car. It wasn't long before they were in clear waters when Simon asked the young man his name.

"I am Adonis." His English was poor and just barely understandable Simon asked him how long before we get there, Adonis looked at him, Simon made a waving motion with his hands. "Októ óres apó tin Thálassa."

"8 óres dia thalássis kai 4 óres me to aftokínito kai téssera óres me to aftokínito."

Simon looked at him then turned to Summer shrugging his shoulders, Adonis then said, "OK, I see what you ask."

Simon looked back at him. "We do eight hours sea then four hours car yes." Showing Simon the map of the bay called Porto Rafti then making a hand gesture saying. "We go very fast." They both settled back into their seats for the long ride but with a sense of relief that they were finally off Rhodes.

The time was now around 7 o'clock in the morning when Marianne finally got a call from Bailey.

"I'm in the main harbour, where are you?"

Marianne looked out from her window; she could just see the harbour from there. "I'm only 15 minutes away from you can you see the small café bar in front of you?"

"Yes," Bailey said.

"I'll see you there in 15 minutes. Get me a coffee, I need it."

Bailey smiled as she finally walked around the corner. "I have your coffee." Marianne sat down opposite him as Bailey said, "So, where are they?"

"I don't know, I've looked all over and have asked around, but nobody knows or they're not saying."

Bailey took a sip of his coffee. "Are you sure they're here?"

"Yes."

"How do you know?"

"Because I know, that's all." There was still no love lost between them.

"Are you sure they haven't moved on?"

"On to where?"

Bailey put his cup down on the table. "Well, come on, if I wanted to get away and couldn't fly from Rhodes then the next best thing would be to fly from Athens come to think of it, I seen a power boat this morning on my way here, just as we were approaching the harbour and it wasn't hanging around."

Marianne slammed her cup down on the table and then slammed her fists down as well. "Damn, I can't believe this is happening to me."

Bentley pushed back into his chair and looked at her, inside he was delighted. She was getting what she deserved, he thought. It was merited. "If it was me, I would be on the next plane to Athens and then waiting at the airport. If you're going to take them both out, then that's the place to do it but this is your problem now not mine and you're going to have to pick up your passport from the hotel so you can give me a ride back."

The speed boat felt as if it was breaking apart as it hit the water at such a high-speed Adonis put his hand up to Simon showing him an OK sign with his fingers just to reassure him that everything was OK. Rhodes was just a small island in the distance now with nothing but open sea in front of them with shimmering heat hitting their faces.

Marianne was now on her way back. Bailey was sitting at the side of her when her phone rang.

"Yes, no they weren't there. I think they may have got a boat over to Athens."

Bailey interrupted as he smiled jokingly saying, "You do know you're not on hands free."

Marianne looked at him; if she had the energy, she would have kicked him out of the car at high speed but she hadn't slept for two days. "Yes, I'm on my way back to the hotel to get my things and then I'm going to jump on the next flight over to Athens, yes I'll get them at the airport, you have just told me what I have just told you, I have just said I'll finish it at the airport, yes before they get on the flight."

"Where to, Miss Green?"

"You can take me to the office. I have some work to go over."

Charles pulled away slowly from her house. "Will you require me for the day, Miss Green?"

"How do I know that? Just do your job you know, just sit in the car and wait, is that understood? You know, like you're supposed to do."

Charles looked at her through his rear-view mirror she was full of self-importance but also very dangerous especially now, even more so, he pulled up to the office's and once she was inside the building, he rang Teddy.

"Good morning, Charles. Do you have anything for me?"

"Yes, sir."

"Fire away," Teddy said.

Charles continued to say, "Jessica Green had made a call whilst in the car. It looks like the plan is to stop Simon and Summer getting back into England and from what I picked up in the conversation, Jessica Green would prefer if they were both terminated, that way she could bring the whole thing to an end."

Teddy asked him if he was prepared for the 'Unexpected', to which Charles replied, "Yes."

Marianne was now back at the hotel, Bailey walked in front of her into the reception area where his men sat waiting for him with their bags packed, he made a hand gesture to them indicating five minutes and then turned around to Marianne.

"I never really took to you but what's done is done, I suggest you get your things and get away from the hotel for your own safety because while we're still here there's every chance you could be having the same fate as Mr Slimm." He then gave her that knowing look, the look that said he knew what he was talking about. Marianne said nothing she just looked at him then turned and made her way to her room.

Sinclair had made his way through passport control at Athens airport when his phone rang.

"Sinclair."

"Teddy, I've just got through passport control."

"What do you have for me?" Teddy got up from his chair rubbing his leg.

"I have a name for you. Marianne Murphy." He then gave him a description of her. "How do you want me to play this one, Teddy?"

"Even though Jessica has ordered a termination on Simon and Summer, obviously this mustn't happen but I'm not ordering a shoot kill on Marianne. I repeat, I am not ordering a shoot kill. I need her back in the UK, is that understood? I'll need you to call me when you're boarding the plane with her, is that understood?"

"Yes, I understand."

"You're going to be staying at the Tonia's Hotel, your firearm will be waiting at the hotel in the usual way and only to be used in extreme measures, you will also have FNL + OCY, you know what to do with this."

Sinclair stopped at one of the airport kiosks. "OK, Teddy, understood. If you get any more information, of course," Teddy said, "I'll stay in touch but will also call you later when your settled in your room."

Sinclair was now outside the airport; his plan was to first hire a car and leave it in the airport car park next was to book into his hotel and have a well-earned shower and then wait for Teddy's call.

Simon and Summer could now see the coastline of mainland Greece in the distance the shimmering heat made it look like a mirage; it was only when Adonis pointed to the shoreline and said soon be Athens his made Simon realise that their boat journey was finally coming to an end, and as another hour had passed, the speed boat cut its overheating tween engines and was now ticking over as it manoeuvred it's way in to the Rocky bay where a lifeline was tossed to them. Well, that's what it felt like for Simon. At last they were both on solid ground. Simon's body still swaying to the motion of the sea as he stood there looking at Summer, again she took it in her stride, now they had a four-hour drive to contend with, and once again Summer gave an emotional hug his time to Adonis, they were one more step closer to home. Their car was parked at the top of the cliff which in itself was no easy task as they both had to make it up by themselves along the makeshift path, the fine loose gravel made it difficult at times. Simon looked down from the cliff to see Adonis's boat bobbing in the bay below its cargo being carried ashore they were like little ants around a sugar cube and as one carry boxes off another loaded the new cargo on which was destined for the island of Rhodes. Once at the top, they both looked down catching their breath their clothes full of dust and Simon frantically tapping his shoe to release that one little stone the size of a pea that had made his climb even harder.

They were greeted by their Greek driver who spoke excellent English. He politely shook their hands and introduced himself. "My name is Barak, but you can call me Rak if it's easier, the first thing we must do," he said as he opened his boot of his car, to their delight placed in the centre of the boot was a large cool box. Barak opened it to reveal cold wet wipes cold water and bread rolls with various fillings. "I'll give you both 15 minutes to refresh yourselves and then you can eat along the way."

The first thing Summer did was to use the wet wipes to wipe away the now dried sea water that had turned to small white patches salt on her face which felt like a scouring agent against her skin; it felt so good to have cleaned away the salt and now they were sitting in the car with the cool air conditioning on drinking ice cold bottled water.

Summer turned saying to Simon, "This is far better than champagne."

Barak asked, "So, where are we going?" "Athens," Simon said.

"Athens is a big place, do you have anywhere in mind?"

Summer asked for a hotel as close as he could get to the airport preferably low-budget and also did he know of any pawnbrokers near to the hotel. "Yes, there's a place I know called Als."

Summer asked if they could go there first.

Marianne was now out for the hotel and on her way to the airport she was fixed on finishing the job, her career depended on it, her plan was to get to the airport and book a flight out to Athens her only worry was how far in front Mr and Mrs Bay were. Marianne's driving was now somewhat erratic she was now like a swan gliding on top of the water but paddling like hell underneath.

Barak pulled up outside Als pawnbrokers after a three hour journey.

"We are here," he said as he turned to them placing his arm on the back of the front passenger seat. "This is Al's."

It was pointless for them both to go in so Summer decided to go in alone. She was greeted by a heavy man with a bad case of body odour that followed her around the shop. She took long deep breaths and tried to hold it in as she took her watch off her wrist and placed it on the counter in front of him; his eyes lit up like a possessed man. Summer had estimated the watch at around about £8000 give or take a little.

"Is the watch yours?" he said.

"Yes, I have some identification."

"No, I don't need to see that," he said as he placed his sweaty hand on top of hers. Summer politely pulled her hand away wiping it on the back of her leg as she did so. He said,

"€2000."

Summer gasped. "But it's brand new."

"€2000. Take it or leave it."

Simon's head turned sharply to his right as the car door opened unexpectedly. Summer got in she was Furious Simon had seen that look many times before as he reluctantly asked if she was all right she showed him her wrist where the watch had been and then said, "He gave me €2000 and I had no choice but to take it."

Barak turned to her. "We Greeks are not all bad, only a few. I'm sure you have this in England as well."

Summer could only smile. "Yes, you're right. We do. It's been a long day can you take us to the hotel now?" Barak pulled up outside a small supermarket that was only a mile from the airport. "Why have we stopped here?" Summer asked as she shuffle forward in her seat resting her hand on the back of the front passenger seat.

"This is the hotel."

"But it's a supermarket."

"Yes, it's what you call a self-catering hotel. It's on the top floor," he said as he pointed up to the top of the building.

"Can this get any worse," Simon said getting out of the car.

Barak got their flight cases from the boot as Summer tried to give him some money, but he refused.

"Have a safe journey and I'll ring Bernus and let him know you are now safely at your hotel." Simon and Summer walked through the narrow doorway to the supermarket its shelves brimming with goods and as they looked down the long aisle, they could see the counter; it seemed a strange setup.

Once there, Summer asked, "Do you have a room for the night please?"

The old lady looked at her, she just stood there waiting her hair tied back in a bun wearing large, rimmed glasses. Summer then pointed to the keys again saying, "Room. Do you have a room?"

The old lady turned. "Eínai nai." Summer then made hand gestures indicating one room for one night. Again, the old lady said, "Domátio gia mia nýchta," as she held the room key up in front of her, Summer nodded as the old lady moved money around in the till.

"€150."

Summer paid her as she was given a key tied with a piece of string to what looked like a small billiard ball with a hole drilled through it and a number written in black felt tip pen, she was then shown the way.

"You come and go at the door on the side." She then pointed outside. Summer then asked if she could use the telephone again making hand gestures. "Tiléfono," the old lady again pointed outside.

The smell of heavy disinfectant and bleach filled the air as Simon opened the door to their room. Everything was in its place even though it was sparsely furnished and although

Summer had said take us to a low-budget hotel, but this was lower the low. Simon dropped his flight case on to the bed, he would have preferred to have dropped himself on it but first things first he needed to get to a telephone and let Teddy know they were now at the hotel.

Summer did as he did and then said, "I'm coming with you."

As the old lady had said the phone kiosk was just across the road from the shop. Summer had now squeezed in behind Simon her chin resting on the back of his shoulder asking him to pull the phone away from his ear so she could listen in on the conversation.

"Teddy here."

"We're at the hotel about a mile from the airport."

Chapter 8

Simon was now anxious Teddy could tell in his voice but then they had every reason to be even the best would have crumbled by now. Teddy asked him to slow down and start again.

"Were at the hotel. It's about one mile away from the airport."

"OK. Here's what you're going to do. Make your way to the airport be there for midday you both fly out at 3 o'clock in the afternoon."

Simon interrupted him. "Are we not flying tonight. I thought we would be flying tonight."

Teddy told him to calm down and listen. "There's a newspaper stand just as you go in to the airport, go to that person you will then give him your name, that's Simon Rodgers, of course, not Mr bay. In return, he will then give you both your flight tickets." Simon asked, "Why the newspaper stand?"

Teddy explained the reasons why, it was to speed things up as he didn't want them out in the open for too long. "Now I need you both to get back to your hotel and try and get some rest it's going to be a busy day tomorrow."

Teddy then hung-up leaving Simon frantically saying,

"Hello, hello."

Teddy put his mobile phone down on the desk and then picked up the office phone. "Did you know it's all gone wrong. Yes, that's what I said. It's gone wrong. They're hiding up in a hotel near the airport. Yes, they're flying tomorrow at three in the afternoon. No, they're going to be there for midday. OK." He then put his finger on the receiver and then dialled out again. "How are you doing there? Are you in place? Yes, good. Simon and Summer will be at the airport tomorrow at midday. I've told them to be on time, yes, OK, good luck." He then turned and stared out of his office window; the world was now on his shoulders.

Marianne was walking through the arrivals lounge at Athens after her short flight from Rhodes when her phone rang, she knew who it was, it could only be one person.

"I'm just walking through arrivals; how do you know this and more to the point who is the information from? A reliable source. So, who is the source? What do you mean I don't need to know that? I will get to them; trust me they will not be getting on the plane."

Simon and Summer were now back in their room. Simon had picked up some food and bottles of wine from the shop below; they both would have liked nothing better than to eat out away from where they were staying but they just couldn't take the risk of being seen. Summer took the only top from her flight case and washed it in the basin with the hard bar of soap that was placed on the side as Simon looked out from the front window that overlooked the shops and bars on the main road below, everywhere was just opening for the evening. He turned to Summer.

"You OK? Yes, just trying to stay busy."

Simon walked over to where she was standing and squeezed her tightly in his arms. "We're nearly there, nearly home." He was trying to give her some reassurance and trying to reassure himself at the same time.

Marianne was now in one of the taxis that were parked outside the airport. "Where to, please?"

"Your nearest hotel." She didn't say please or thank you; it wasn't in her nature. It took the driver 15 minutes to get to the hotel. After all, Marianne did say the nearest, and this was his choice, but why this one, because he got back handers from hotel's, all the taxi drivers did. Marianne was there now. She opened the door to the hotel as her taxi sped away. It was a hotel bar, a bar where the locals drank, a seedy little place. The door slammed shut behind her as the people at the bar turned to her. Marianne looked at them with disapproving eyes.

"Room for the night." The barman carried on talking not being out done Marianne picked up a barstool and slammed it back down on the floor to get the barman's attention, she now had it. "A room for one night."

"€120."

The money was placed on the bar as he turned to the bored on the wall where he picked a sticky room key and passed it to her, he then passed her a single towel, Marianne's eyes once again said it all he then said as he turned back to the bar.

"Leave the towel here when you go. What a dump," she said under her breath. She was now sat on her bed after checking the bed sheets, at least they were clean. It was now time for her to go through the plans in her head and who to kill first. It had to be Summer as she was in Marianne's eyes the strongest and then do Simon next. Her choice of weapons were knives she had used handguns in the past but found there was too much attention and because of this, she had made the decision to leave her beloved Makarov pistol which she acquired from a worthy adversary. Its black onyx handle and silver-plated barrel would have no doubt given her unnecessary attention and for that reason she had left it in safe hands back at the hotel in Rhodes. Her plan was to go back and collect it once Simon and Summer were out of the way, and anyway knives were quieter. She had decided on one stab to the neck where it meets the shoulder from behind forcing the blade downwards and then pulling the person back. She would then step to the left hand-side then swinging her arm out and around and piercing the heart as she fell. The second kill would be easier as he would be that mortified as to what had just happened and undoubtedly be kneeling next to her with this in mind she would strike two blows into his side and then sending the final strike to his femoral artery leaving him to bleed out, quick and simple, and then just walk away through the crowd. Marianne practiced the move a couple of times and then opened her case. She didn't unpack what was the point. She just moved her clothes to one side and pulled out a black velvet box the size of a shoe box; this was Marianne's box of tricks. She placed the box on the bed carefully, caressing it before it was opened to reveal four hair brushes. She moved the palm of her hand gently across them. To anybody else, they were four barrel brushes, nothing on towards there, well not to prying eyes, but each one of them was special to her in its own way. She picked one up by the bristle barrel and with her other hand, she held the handle tightly and then pushed it down in to the barrel turning the handle sharply to the left. Then there was a click as the spring released mechanism allowing her to pull the handle out of the barrel revealing a blade which was very similar to a fillet knife, the blade itself was made from very hard and durable plastic which was sharper and stronger then steel, and more importantly this was something Marianne could take through the airport security undetected, each of the different size brushes had a knife inside. Marianne then lifted the tray from the box to reveal four knife pouches with Velcro straps, again each one was the size of the knife brushes. She put one of the pouches on the top of her arm and then slipped the knife into its place. This then rested in between the top of her arm and the elbow. She then put her jacket on to conceal it. Once again, she went through the motion, pulling the brush knife from inside the top sleeve of her jacket and then replacing the brush knife back in to its place. She had this to perfection, it was perfect. She often thought how beautiful these knives were, the fact that she could end somebody's life and then brush her hair afterwards, sick, she caressed them again and again. All Marianne could do now was wait. She had time on her hands, they all had time on their hands.

Sinclair was sat in the hotel restaurant eating lobster tails and drinking Dom Perignon Vintage, Simon and Summer were sat at the window watching the world go by and deep in thought. Marianne was still pulling the knife out from her jacket, practice makes perfect. Judgement Day or was it to be Simon's and Summer's escape back to the safety of England only time would tell, as the sun raised on their final day in Athens they were both sat up in bed, they didn't have much sleep and what sleep they had was with one eye open. Simon found it such a big effort just to put his feet on the floor in front of him, the past three days had just caught up with them both. The curtains were closed in Sinclair's room blocking out the sunlight this was just another day to him. He was always ready for the unexpected, his gun place at his side in bed not under his pillow as they do in the films. It was easier to get to when it was at his side, all this was in a day's work for him after all this was his profession but nevertheless, it was now personal because it was Simon, the same Simon who nearly lost his life rather than give the names of The Fat Club up.

Marianne was sat in the corner of her room, just sat there looking at the ceiling light whilst twisting the ring around on her finger. As the morning moved on, the time was now right for Simon and Summer to make their move. The room key was placed on the shop counter the old lady waved from the back of the shop saying, "Antio sas."

Simon waved back smiling at her and as he did, so he said to Summer, "We're going to have to learn Greek for when we come back because I didn't understand a word she said." Getting a taxi at that time of day was quite difficult it being a small place and all, nobody really knew it existed it was only really for the local people but their perseverance eventually paid off. Simon jumped in first. "To the airport, please."

Summer interrupted him, and then asked the taxi driver is it possible to be dropped off near the main gate not actually at it, the driver looked around at them before setting off.

"Yes, no problem."

"Why?" Simon asked as they travelled towards the airport.

"We're not sure if we're alone, are we?"

"Right," Simon said in an inquisitive way.

Summer carried on to say, "If we get out of the car away from the main gate, then if there is anybody waiting for us then at least we'll have a chance of getting away and most of all staying alive."

Simon looked out of the car window. Will this ever end.

By this time, Marianne was already at the airport waiting, she had checked out of her hotel early that morning her case placed for safe keeping at the car rental close by she had told them she was going to wait for some relatives at the airport and then come back for her case and rent a car from them for the week, this was Marianne's way out. This was her escape plan after killing them both.

The taxi pulled up to a stop not too far away from the main gate Summer looked up towards the doors as Simon said, "How do we know who's who?"

Summer answered him, "We don't, but hopefully we will notice them in good time." They slowly got out of the car as if they knew they were going to their deaths, they both slowly walked up to the main door's cases in their hands, this was it. Marianne spotted them from a distance, she had been waiting at the corner of the building for some time, waiting for this moment and this was it, it was now or never, she made her way towards them quickly covering ground behind them she undone the button on her jacket her knife at the ready and now making ready her right hand for the first attack on Summer.

"Nearly there," Simon said. "Nearly home and dry." Marianne was now less than ten metres away, she now slowly pulled the knife from the inside of jacket sleeve and then slowly put her arm down to her side as not to draw any unwanted attention to herself. The knife waiting to do its job and finally put her in the clear, her knife was now at arm's length ready to do the job ready to finish it once and for all. Simon was only five metres away from the main door. As it opened automatically, he waited behind the crowd of people jostling to get their place in line, they were almost there, they could now feel the cool air of the air-conditioning on their faces when Simon was quickly and unexpectedly pushed forward. He looked around as he was losing his balance only to see Summer being push against him, in his mind this was it, it was over, there was a scuffle only to see Summer picking him up as he nearly hit the ground, breaking his fall, there's something going on outside we need to get in out of the way, what's happened Simon said as Summer steadied him, there was some sort of disturbance outside. Once inside the airport, they both stood within the safety of the people standing in queues for their flight's home that was when Summer pointed over to the newspaper stand, they both knew they had to leave the safety of the Crowd and walk across the open space to get to it, but when. Their walk was slow and steady every step they took their hearts missed a beat.

Once there, Summer said, "Hello?"

He didn't reply, not a word did he say.

Summer turned to Simon. "Have we got the right person?"

"What did Teddy say to us?" In all the confusion, they had both forgotten, then Simon realised.

He remembered, he looked at Summer and then back at the person. "My name is Simon Rodgers." They waited as the person looked at them both as he put his hand in to his inside pocket. Simon put his arm across the front of Summer to try and keep her safe from harm not knowing what was going to happen next but then, to their relief, they saw the flight tickets being pulled from his pocket, it was as quick as that. He passed them to Simon and then vanished into the waiting crowd. They now had their tickets and there was no hanging around.

Teddy was sat at the bar at the golf club when his phone rang.

"Teddy here, are good then they both got out all right. But did you see them? Good that's fantastic news, and do you have her? Is she still alive? Good. Do you have anything at all to tell me? No? Say again. You will by tonight, good news I look forward to hearing from you, goodbye."

Sinclair put his phone down as he turned to Marianne, he had her tied to the chair in his hotel room. Her legs were strapped to the two front legs of the chair and her arms tied behind her back. Sinclair always packed four belts in his case for such an occasion. The fourth belt was somewhat shorter than the other leather belts, and that one was tight around her mouth. Sinclair gave her a light slap across her face again and again to bring her around. Marianne forced her head back struggling with the reality that she now realised she was tied to a chair.

"Your name is Marianne, is it not? A simple nod of the head will suffice." She stared back at him. "Is your name Marianne?" She swallowed deeply her throat dry. Sinclair picked up the syringe. "It's the injection I gave you. Let me remind you, you looked very professional out there, but you forgot the golden rule. 'When you're chasing somebody, you should always look around you to see who's chasing you'. Is your name Marianne?" Her anger was now beginning to show. "You do know you failed and they're now on a plane back to England, so therefore, you didn't achieve what you were sent out to do, did you? Is your name Marianne?"

She put her head down slightly.

"Do you work for Jessica Green?"

Marianne's head raised back up, it was a dead giveaway, again Sinclair asked her. "Is your name Marianne? I have all the time in the world but I must warn you when I get bored I will finish you in the chair where you are now with no dignity, so it's time to think about your family. Think about the last time you saw them because this will be the last time you ever think of them again. Now, I'll say this again. Is your name Marianne?"

Her head dropped down again as Sinclair walked over to the chest of drawers, her head was up now trying to look in front of him to see what he was getting. He then turned with something in his hand but she couldn't see what it was, she frantically struggled in the chair unsure of what was to come. Sinclair raised his hand as he got closer to her, Marianne's eyes opened wide, Sinclair could see the fear within them. "Let me tell you something about Jessica Green, you know, the lady you work for." Marianne looked at him, Sinclair showed her a phone that he had picked up from the chest of drawers. "Jessica is ruthless and dangerous as well and she has no respect for others, only for herself. She was moved up to your organisation. What it's called I don't know but we will get to that later if you decide to help us, did you know Jessica intended to send you to your death after the job. Have I got your attention now?"

Marianne nodded once.

"Good. She was going to send you back to the hotel in Rhodes telling you everything was cleared up and you would be going back in under cover but what she was really doing was tidying up the loose ends." Sinclair looked at her. "You don't believe me I get that, if I was in your place, I think I wouldn't either. I would be thinking the way you're thinking now."

Sinclair moved his phone towards Marianne's ear. She pulled away as he did so. "I know you don't believe me that's why I want you to listen to this conversation between Jessica and an unknown person." He played it to her.

"Is everything in order?"

"Yes, sir."

"How did he die then?"

"I'm not sure, sir."

"Who are these people that are impersonating Mr and Mrs Bay?"

"I know who they are sir, and there wasn't going to be a problem I had intended to use them as bait to get Marianne even closer to Mr Slimm."

"So what went wrong?"

"He died, sir."

"This is not good. What do you intend to do to put it right?"

"I've already sent my agent to get rid of them. I've told her they must not get back to England."

"And what about your agent? You know she is a risk to you now."

"Yes, sir, I told her to ring me when the job is done, my intentions are to send her back to Rhodes where Mr Slimm's men will finish the job for me."

"Good, so you have everything in hand I wouldn't want you to lose your job over this."

"No, sir, it's all in hand."

Marianne's shoulders dropped as she put her head down in shame again. Sinclair picked up on this, your name is Marianne is it not again she looked up at him but this time she nodded, now he knew he had broken her.

Simon and Summer were now flying somewhere over

France. It was a low budget flight, the first flight they could get, but what did they care at least they were out of danger.

Simon looked out of the window as Summer read the inflight magazine.

Sinclair now had Marianne's attention. "If I take the belt from around your mouth, will you stay quiet and listen?"

She nodded her head in agreeance. Marianne moved her jaw up and down to rid the ache and to relieve indentations around her cheekbones. "I have to take you back to England but there's two ways we can do this. I think you already know the first one and I don't think you would last long back home do you."

Marianne asked him what's the second option.

"First of all, you ring Jessica Green and tell her the job's done. Do this first."

Marianne agreed.

"I'm going to untie you and what you do next is up to you.

the door is unlocked so if you decide to run you can do but if you do you know you're a dead person."

She decided to stay. "Give me the phone."

Jessica was sat at her desk when her phone rang. "Yes, I'm here, what do you have for me? So it's done. Where did it happen? Was it in public? Good. Where are you now? Good. No, don't fly back to England it's now calmed down in Rhodes, so I want you to get back there and stay under cover.

Yes, that's what I said, Rhodes."

Marianne slammed the phone down on the table shaking with anger her adrenaline was now pumping around her body. Sinclair calmed her down.

"What would you say if I asked you to come and work for the Fat Club?"

"Why?" she said.

"Because we could do with somebody like you."

Marianne was all ears what else did she have to lose?

After all, Jessica had made it quite clear she was a risk now.

"Go on, tell me more."

Sinclair sat down at the table next to her.

"First of all, what is the department you work for?"

"It's called P4."

"What do they do?"

"They infiltrate and acquire secret information and then act on it."

"Who is your boss?"

"I honestly don't know. I've worked for them now for four years and have never spoke to the person."

"So how did you become to be in P4?"

"My commanding officer in the special forces told me I was being moved up, have you heard of the Fat Club?"

"Yes, but only rumours."

"Right, well my boss would like you to work for us through your department."

"You mean pass you information?"

"Yes, if that's what you want to call it."

"And what do I get out of it?"

“A job, you get to keep your job and of course you get to make a lot of money, oh and one last thing, you get to see

Jessica Green go down.”

“That bit I like, but how would you do it if she has already spoken to the person.”

“You leave that to us.” Sinclair then said, “So there’s the door, do you run, but then that would mean you would be on the run for the rest of your life, always looking over your shoulder for people like me, or do you take my advice and work for us?”

Without hesitation, she answered, “I’m on board.”

“Good, I need to go down to the reception to arrange two flights back to England. Am I OK to leave you alone?” Marianne nodded.

“Do I have your word?”

Teddy’s phone rang, he answered it quickly, “Teddy here, is it good news? So as far as Jessica Green knows Simon and Summer are now dead. So what’s her name? Right, so her name is Marianne. It’s just that I’ve never heard of her before. Good, and you were there when she told Jessica Green. Good at least Simon and Summer won’t be in any danger when they arrive back in the UK. I’ll have a man there waiting for them. Is she on board then? Good, get her back here make sure she doesn’t contact anybody. Yes, come straight to The Fat Club. Thank you, goodbye.”

Sinclair opened the door to his room only to find Marianne wasn’t there. Had she had a change of heart? Had he made a mistake? This wasn’t like him, he was normally a good choice of character, he walked over to the window wondering what to do next when he saw her. She was walking back to the hotel with her case. She’d been over to the car rental. Sinclair opened the room door and sat down waiting for her.

Simon and Summer were now walking through arrivals not knowing what to do next when a man approached them.

"Mr and Mrs Rodgers, I'm your driver, follow me."

Simon stopped and stood his ground; he had now had enough of this. "This stops here where not going anywhere with you, who are you anyway."

The person stepped back away from him and dialled out on his mobile phone. "Sir, they're not getting in the car. Yes sir." He passed his phone over to Simon. "He would like to speak to you."

To Simon's delight, it was Teddy. "Simon, the driver is friendly. He's there to get you and Summer out of there. We're going to get you both to the hotel where you both did your identity swap, do you remember? You will be debriefed once you're there."

Simon gave the driver his phone back then said to Summer, "Let's go." It was an uncomfortable drive to the hotel as in the way that they hadn't really washed for three days it was that bad they could smell their own body odour. Summer had given up on a bad job with her hair. It now resembled plaited string, or as Simon would say rattails, that was something he would normally joke about but not now. They were both on familiar ground as the driver pulled up to the front of the hotel. Last time they had seen this place was the early hours of the morning on their way out and it seemed a lifetime ago. The driver opened the car door as they got out now tired and exhausted. They met the same hotel receptionist as before but he didn't recognise them, but then he wouldn't have. Simon asked for the key.

"Mr and Mrs Rodgers, you have a room for us." The receptionist passed them the key, room 9.

Simon opened the door pushing it back allowing Summer to enter first, she was startled when she entered Simon pulled her back only to see someone sat at the table, it was Joseph.

"Hello, Simon, you had us all worried. It's good to see you."

Simon held his hand out as Joseph got up to greet him, "This is my wife, Summer."

After the pleasantries, Joseph explained to them both that he was the one who would be debriefing them. "It's better to have someone you know," he carried on to say, "I've took the liberty of ordering you some food it will be delivered to your room as well as wine and beer, as we didn't know what size you both are, we've put some relaxed t-shirts and pants in the bedroom for you, your food will arrive in one hour that should give you both time to freshen up, but I must insist that we do the debrief tonight this is very important to us and most of all it's what's best for you." Joseph then left a mobile phone on one of the small tables in the room. "My number is in the phone it's the only number so when you're ready, ring me, I'll speak to you soon, try and enjoy your food."

There was a silence in the room as Joseph closed the door behind him. Summer was the first in the shower she just stood there the hot water running down her body in a way it was cleansing away the pain and stress she had been put through. Simon was frantically cleaning his teeth with the small plastic toothbrush supplied by the hotel. He stood there thinking to himself these are the things you take for granted.

Eventually, Summer reluctantly got out of the shower, she had her smile back, now it was Simon's turn, they looked like death warmed up but at least now they were clean. There was a knock on the door Simon looked through the peephole both palms of his hands pressed against the door ecstatically saying, "Yes, food's here. At last, some proper food." Summer could only smile at him as he opened the door, four bags to be precise with wine and beer as promised, it was the best food ever; they hadn't really eaten for the three days only bits along the way. Just over two hours had passed when Simon said, "We really need to get this debriefing over with." Summer agreed as Simon picked up the phone and called him.

"Hello, Simon, are you ready for me now?"

"Yes, how long will it take you to get here?"

Joseph explained to him that it would only take five minutes as he was in the same hotel. "You both look much better," Joseph said as he was let into their room by Summer. "But I would shoot your tailor." That broke the ice as they all started to laugh as Joseph sat them down on the two-seater in the corner of their room as he opened a brown folder. "This is just your debriefing. Firstly, how are you both?" Joseph watched for their reaction. Their response to the question, Simon said he was glad it was all over but Summer didn't say a word. Joseph marked it down on the relevant piece of paper he then asked more questions about how they were feeling before asking how Mr Slimm died they both told him everything he needed to know, how he died, how they fled from the hotel, about the family who helped them escape and got them over to Athens, about the telephone number on the ring and when they rang the number for help that's when all hell broke loose, but then to Joseph's astonishment they knew nothing about what had happened at the airport. He made sure they were comfortable before continuing to say. "You didn't know of the compromising situation you were both in at the airport." They both looked at each other. "I have to tell you as part of your debriefing that Marianne was at the airport, did you notice any disturbance at the main doors?" Simon said yes, but in an inquisitive way.

"Marianne was sent to kill you both, her orders were to make sure you didn't make it back to England, she very nearly succeeded only for Sinclair taking her down at the airport on the orders of Teddy."

Simon asked, "So, is she dead then?"

Joseph answered him, "NO."

Summer's eyes welled up not because she was still alive. No Summer wasn't the least interested in her now, it was because now she felt as if she was now finally a part of the team because until now, she felt as if they had both been left out to dry.

Teddy was in his office at home when he got the call, he'd been waiting for. "Thank you for ringing me at this late hour."

"You're welcome," Sinclair said as he continued to say, "We have someone who wishes to defect from their organisation. Yes, sir, from P4 or you may know it as Phoenix 4. Yes, sir, she would be an asset to The Fat Club. Yes, sir, of her own free will. Yes, sir, but we have a problem in the way that she has been told to go back out under cover with the likelihood that there's a shoot kill on her. No, sir, I don't want to lose her. Yes, sir, Jessica Green. Thank you, sir. Yes, sir, we're at the airport, we should be back in England around five in the morning sir. Yes, that will get us to The Fat Club around eight a.m. Yes, sir, we will see you there. Thank you, sir."

Joseph was now coming to the end of his debriefing, the brown folder was put away in to his briefcase, as for Simon and Summer, it was all over for them now, they just sat there speechless as Joseph said his final words, "I would like to thank you on behalf of The Fat Club for all your hard work, in the next couple of days you will receive some documents through the post I would like you to go through them if you would, Simon you will then hand them in to Teddy." Summer stood up.

"What?"

"Is that it?" Yet again she felt so let down, only moments ago she felt needed, now she felt they had been pulled from pillar to post only now to be told that was it.

A week had past, and everything was running as normal, Marianne was now back at P4, gathering information for The Fat Club, Teddy to show loyalty and appreciation had given the order to one of his agents to collect Marianne's Makarov pistol from the hotel in Rhodes on his way through. Jessica Green got her comeuppance as Teddy knew she would he had always said she was too eager. She was stripped of any authority and blamed for the failure of the mission even though Mr Slimm died of natural causes, but now within the organisation, she wasn't to be trusted as it was now common knowledge that she was willing to send agents to their death to save her own skin. She was put out of arms way working for Oliver and Jack in the technical department as a filing clerk with watchful eyes on her every move. Simon was back at work doing what he did best and swore he would never get him or Summer into that situation again, and of course, Teddy agreed.

As for Summer, well, she was back to normal and back at work, it had been a world wind but there it was; it was now finished, and now she was sat at a table with her uniform on the badge on her lapel saying Summer Rodgers, occupational therapist, having a morning cup of tea when she was asked, "So, how was your holiday? Was the weather nice and is it a place you would go again?"

Summer could only smile as she put her cup down on the table in front of her and thought for a moment before saying, "Maybe, who knows. If the price is right then maybe I would go again, I suppose."

"But have you had time to think about my offer?"

Summer said, "Yes, I have." She was sat in front of Teddy in his office. "I have thought about it long and hard, and the answer is yes."

"Good news," Teddy said, "it's good to have you on the team," as he opened the file. "As you know, you will still be working as an occupational therapist as part of your cover for The Fat Club, and will go on courses representing your job when we need you to do some work for us, the money side of it, won't be a problem as we are looking at raising your husband's tender, this will stop any suspicion of extra money going into your account. Obviously, Simon must never know about this arrangement." Summer agreed.

"We're going to set up a bogus online account so when we need to get in touch with you. This will link up to your mobile phone you will see it as sunlight holidays, we will contact you through this company." Teddy then pushed a piece of paper across the table to her. "Just something for you to sign, I think you know what it is."

Joseph walked in just as Summer had pen to paper, Teddy walked over to the window with him out of earshot as Joseph showed him a document and then said, "This could be it, sir. But we do now have a small problem, as the Russians are involved, our intelligence have informed us that they're sending four agents in from the F.S.B."

Teddy looked at him patting him on the shoulder as he then turned to Summer saying, "My dear, have you ever been to Oxford?"

The End

Ingram Content Group UK Ltd.
Milton Keynes UK
UKHW020638220623
423865UK00011B/586

9 781398 424289